OBJECTION

ANDRE SANDERS

Dedicated to Addiction
2000-2022
Burn in Hell.

For my parents
Larry & Rebecca Sanders

My siblings
Stephanie & Justin Sanders

These two have been nothing but loving and supportive. They've shown me life can be fun without substance.

A special friend
Brandy Steele

Thank you for being understanding, supportive, and not judgemental during my darkest time. You are awesome!

CHAPTER ONE

Shei Rivera looked in the rearview mirror after parking the vehicle and watched the young child - approximately seven years old - with the same long dark color hair, tug a cute puppy design book bag onto her lap while trying to unfasten the seat belt also. She struggled for a bit with the backpack because it was nearly as big as her, which made unfastening the buckle slightly more difficult than usual.

"Got your homework, squirt?" Shei asked.

"Yeah," the child replied, finally freeing herself from the restraint.

"Lunch box?" Shei inquired.

"Rocky ate it," the kid uttered, scooting from the middle of the backseat and making her way to the passenger door.

Shei smiled upon hearing the response and nothing more had to be mentioned because she knew the box was in the bag. Rocky was the name of the furry backpack perfectly designed for a child. Actually, it could probably be altered into a stuffed animal if a child desired that it be one. Having floppy ears sewn on the sides, large blue plastic eyes, and a small brown plastic nose glued on the smaller front zip pocket, the shoulder bag resembled a toy more than an actual school accessory.

"Love you, sweetheart. Have a good day," she said.

The little girl struggled opening the door on the SUV and succeeded only by pushing with one of her scrawny legs.

"Love you, mommy," she expelled in one breath.

The child jumped out of the vehicle and slammed the door shut. Shei peered out the front passenger window and did not see her daughter again until she stepped away with her back toward the vehicle and continued on the sidewalk leading to the elementary school. Spanning the length and width of her back, the makeshift pet puppy was difficult for her to contend with based on how it hunched her forward and wilted her shoulders. Realistically, the wooly packsack was intended for a child some years ahead of first-grade; however, this kid fell in love when she saw it, and being the type of mom who made certain her little one was always happy, Shei didn't think twice about doing what was necessary to please her.

A group of older children - presumably sixth or seventh graders given their size - emerged on the sidewalk. As the risk of losing sight of the tiniest child in the crowd escalated, Shei tapped the horn briefly. The girl turned, smiling, while squinting to block sunlight from obstructing her view. She raised one arm halfway in the air and quickly waved. Without waiting to witness if her mother would return the gesture, she spun forward and suddenly vanished inside the hive of older kids approaching the school entrance. The last glimpse of her that Shei caught involved seeing the backpack give a farewell of its own by the droopy ears flapping wildly when she turned.

Assuming her daughter walked inside the school

with the wave of other students, Shei turned to the driver's window and looked as far behind her side as she could see before shifting the gear in *Drive* and carefully progressing away from the designated pupil drop-off.

Her routine commute on Interstate 81 was always onerous; not only because it was congested by locals but also by people from surrounding counties that worked in Roanoke. Another obstacle was the fact that the state highway department seemed to constantly have some major project underway that apparently began at the crack of dawn. This morning wasn't inconsistent with her ordinary experiences - except it was busier. The state department was paving the right side of the southbound lane; therefore, all traffic was cautiously diverted into the left lane. She felt like she wasn't going anywhere most of the time since traffic was heavily backed up and barely creeping along.

She glanced in the rearview mirror and saw the massive grill of a tractor trailer right up on her ass. If for any reason she had to slam on the brakes, then she was positive she would kiss her back bumper goodbye. Checking the mirror and getting a half view of the backseat also reminded her that she was the lone occupant inside the vehicle. She practically forgot about no longer having the little person with her because the traffic situation gave her instant stress and scattered her thoughts everywhere but in the moment.

She sighed, thinking how much better things would be if she just relaxed.

Then she reached down and pressed the power button on the stereo system. Music blasted from the speakers, so loud that she could almost feel the door panel vibrate to the split-second instrumental opening of the song. The gruff southern accent in a man's voice started spitting audio. His colorful vocabulary may have been the reason she didn't have it playing in the company of her daughter. Keeping one hand off the wheel, she slung various gestures as if she was a veteran in the rap game. In reality, she might be embarrassed if someone she was close and dear with saw her cutting loose since her resemblance to a sophisticated real estate broker didn't quite fit well with this behavior. The track *On That* was one of her all time favorites, and the artists La Chat, Gangsta Boo, and Lil Wyte were amongst the handful of performers she listened to regularly.

She drew a deep breath.

"Rock out with my cock out!" she yelled, drowning out Lil Wyte rapping the phrase.

Afterwards, she giggled at her own silliness. Maybe this amusement involved her finding humor in mentioning having a penis since she obviously didn't have one.

BA- LOO- LOO- LOOB.

BA- LOO- LOO- LOOB.

"Fucking overkill!" she griped, having the personally uplifting jam unexpectedly disrupted by an incoming call transferred from her phone to the vehicle via bluetooth.

The touchscreen on the stereo system showed the name of the contact - *Asshole (Dad)* - attempting to reach her. Shei growled reproachfully. For whatever reason, she appeared not too thrilled about the unanticipated distraction.

She tapped the box labeled *Accept* and the ringing ceased. "Hi, daddy," she greeted, surprisingly pulling off an impression that she was excited.

"Hey, sugar plum. Have you dropped Sierra off at school already?" His booming voice came at her from all directions.

"Yes. Now I'm stuck in this crap on 81. It never fails; every morning, the state is doing something to cause havoc," she proclaimed.

"Well... You are about to catch yourself a little break. Speaking of, are you ready for the trip?" he asked.

"Not at all," she spouted. "I've got no idea where I'm staying and I'm uncertain how things are going to go. To be honest, I'm not even sure that I want to go."

"Oh, Shei. You are going to be fine. It's only a three-day trip. The time will fly. I did reserve a few special arrangements for you. The most important thing to me is your bedding. I made damn certain that you have your own space, and clean lenins. Definitely clean lenins. God only knows what all goes on in those beds," he said.

"Gross!" she commented, laughing.

"I'm serious, Shei," he said assertively. *"You don't want to be rolling around in stains or pubic hairs."*

She shook her head, and the smile quickly sank almost into a frown. "Okay. I'll remember that, I guess."

"All that you've got to do is keep your head up. Focus on your responsibilities, and sweep whatever bullshit under the rug. You are intelligent and have always done what you set your mind to doing. Go in with the right attitude and you'll come out of there eminently rewarded. Think of it as a job - requiring you to do what is necessary

to earn a decent paycheck," he mentioned.

"I'm not worried about getting the job done," she fired back. "My only concern is Sierra. Like, I need to know she is going to be okay."

"Did you tell her that you have a business trip to attend?" he inquired.

"No, I did not!" she exclaimed. "She would've been all to pieces if I said anything to her, and probably wouldn't be in school right now. She's very partial to me. You know how she is."

"She's like a little guard dog," he said, laughing. *"But you don't have to worry about Sierra. I'll keep her entertained for the next several days. I do have court tomorrow, so Beatrice will be picking her up from school."*

"I thought you were getting rid of her?" she asked, suddenly hitting the brakes when the vehicle in front of her stopped abruptly.

"I was ready to let her go but she's one mean chef. Other than cooking, she tidies the place up nicely," he commented.

"Oh- Well… It's nice you have her to look after you still," she remarked.

Her father coughed and its cruddy rattle reverberated throughout the vehicle. *"You're positive that you're okay with doing this?"* he asked.

Shei grimaced in a way potentially expressing uncertainty. Fortunately, her father could not distinguish doubt since she obviously practiced having her voice elude it. "Yeah, I'm good to go. Things will get better once I've settled in and understand exactly what I'm up against. Not knowing what to expect is all that's got me nervous."

"I can tell you right now that this is not going to be a simple task. Truthfully, I do regret getting you involved but there really isn't anyone I can trust to take on the engagement."

"How bad can three days be, right?" she publicized, eventually catching a break in traffic by swerving into the right lane following the end of roadwork. "The most difficult part will be not seeing my baby girl and kissing her goodnight before bed."

"It's going to be hard on all of us, but I've got faith in you," he admitted.

Shei lingered, momentarily silent, upon the threshold of critical thinking. She was exceptionally concerned about the duties ahead of her but she couldn't address the issue to her father because he'd only worry constantly and deny Sierra the attention that she deserved.

"I don't expect to be in touch any time soon, so I guess I'll reach out after the job is finalized," she said, flipping her signal before merging onto the right side exit ramp.

"Call me as soon as you get the opportunity," he insisted.

"I'll do that. Also, will you give Sierra a kiss for me?" she asked, fighting not to get choked up.

"Yes, honey. I'll be sure to give her your bedtime smooches."

"Love you, dad," she spoke softly.

"I love you too, sugar plum. Be careful out there."

Shei took those to be his final words and ended their conversation. The music picked up thumping where it left off but wasn't uplifting anymore. She could not hold back the sorrow of leaving her daughter behind for any longer. Heartache seeped from her eyes while she focused on the road made blurry by crying.

Before today, she genuinely believed that she had mentally toughened herself for the business event.

Now, with the trip looming and all contact with her family - most importantly Sierra - obsolete, she felt overwhelmingly unprepared.

Shei Rivera really didn't know what she was getting herself into.

CHAPTER TWO

The cul de sac was peaceful during the mornings; of course, Shei considered it to be very relaxed in the evenings as well. The most commotion anyone had to deal with was the handful of kids that came out to play. They were always riding their bicycles, playing hide and seek, tossing frisbee, and sometimes they'd all come together for a game of hopscotch at the center of the cul de sac. There were only five children total, including Sierra. Their ages ranged from four to eleven. Shei enjoyed having more children in the vicinity because they kept Sierra entertained and held her lonesomeness at bay since she didn't have siblings.

What Shei enjoyed most about living in the cul de sac was that everyone - of course, there were only six houses - knew each other by name. She didn't have to worry about Sierra going outside and getting approached by some random stranger. When they lived in downtown Roanoke, she hardly allowed Sierra to go out. Then again, there wasn't anyplace for her to hang out; they lived roughly half a mile from the city park. Living on the outskirts of the suburbs was the best thing that could have happened to them after her nasty split from an emotionally abusive piece of shit, who was also Sierra's father. The cul de sac provided a way of life that she never dreamed was possible. Neighbors were friendly. The atmosphere was calm. They were in a safe location. She couldn't ask for a better place to raise Sierra.

She snatched her phone from the cupholder in the center console dividing the driver and passenger seats. Hustling the short distance across the lawn, she stepped onto the small concrete slab of an unsheltered porch and sprung the storm door open before quickly pursuing the wooden one. Presumably she had a lot of trust in the neighbors because she opened the door without having to unlock it first. Going forward, she stepped into a decently decorated dining area. Apparently, she had a fascination with peacocks since there was a large oil painting of one on the wall and a vase on the dining table with a variety of feathers sticking out.

She shut the door behind her and went toward-

"Sonuvabitch!" she shrieked, stopping and leaning forward before crossing her leg on her stomach.

Wobbling on one leg with no sense of balance, she grabbed the last two small toes on her raised foot. A few quick gasps accompanying the displeased facial expression insinuated that she was experiencing some level of hurt.

Shei looked at the floor and spotted the well camouflaged culprit that she had barely clipped was a tiny dark Lego block laying upside down.

"Goddammit, Sierra," she griped, continuing to hold her toes.

Finally, the initial pain subsided and she put her foot down. One sudden jolt of that same foot and she kicked the Lego so far out of the way that it slid under the table. She stepped forward with barely any difficulty but a vague difference in how her other foot stepped did show that there was still a trace amount of agitation.

Before the misfortunate ordeal involving that damn building block, Shei had a pretty good notion about the first thing she was going to do after dropping Sierra off at school. Unfortunately, she lost track of all things in her agenda after acquiring this temporarily mild discomfort.

Approaching the spacious entryway which provided a view of just the sofa and coffee table in the living room, she contemplated memorizing a completely new list of things to do by order of importance.

"Clothes!" she blurted out, pausing only a few steps away from reaching the entryway.

Something the majority of people didn't know about her was that she'd occasionally talk to herself. Didn't matter the nature of the circumstance, Shei would think something and then answer her thought aloud.

When clothes came to mind, she remembered having laundry in the dryer from last night that needed to be folded and put away.

Ready to tackle her responsibilities on this predetermined clusterfuck of a day, she was suddenly and completely grasped by horror when her partial view of the living room became abruptly overtaken by pure whiteout.

Shei screamed but the sound proved incapable of fleeing her mouth because the plastic bag was pulled tightly against her face. There wasn't enough slack for the bag to swell when she breathed, and there was a lot of expiring taking place since she was in absolute panic. Whoever this uninvited perpetrator was that pulled the bag over her head, they were instantly successful in asphyxiating her.

She grabbed her throat and tried ripping the plastic but her attacker had such strength that she couldn't grip the bag because it was so tight-fitting that the sleek material felt as though it became her skin. Failing to yank it off her head, Shei raised one hand to her mouth and sank her fingernails into the plastic until she managed to tear a tiny hole. She sucked as much as she could get but felt that every little bit was not sufficient enough since she had gone for too long without.

The intruder must have been knowledgeable of her designing the airway because they directed one leg in front of both her legs and aggressively sprung to action. Shei fell forward once her feet got snatched backwards and out from under her. Slamming frontwards on the floor knocked every bit of preserved air out of her while the intruder laid on top, pressing all of their stout weight to pin her effectively transfixed. The only thing she could do in her defense was scratch the floor which literally did nothing to help her get anywhere. She could not fight off her attacker. Couldn't scream. Regrettably, her only option was to remain situated and undergo whatever degree of distress that her aggressor desired to inflict.

Getting suffocated had gone on for some time, but Shei just now recognized that she was disoriented. Even if she was in a better position to put up a struggle, she would not have the physical assurance to protect herself based on being severely discombobulated.

Just when she thought the intruder only had plans to smother her, the individual raised her head off the floor. The one thought going through her mind was that she was very thankful that Sierra wasn't home to witness or experience this fierce assault, because there was no telling what a vicious individual might do to a child. Disregarding her own despondence, she held onto her appreciation that Sierra was out of harm's way. Strangely, this margin of gratefulness somehow mentally displaced her from the situation enough to lessen the rigidity of things affecting her emotionally.

She wished that her attacker would finish whatever they anticipated but do so while sparing her life, and that hefty weight bearing down on top of her incontinently reacted as if it was a god that read her mind. She didn't see it coming but she definitely felt the consequence of having the side of her face impinge upon the floor. An immediate pain thrashed from her chin up to her cheekbone beneath the eye socket, and then it spanned further to throb inside the anterior temporal area of her head. The unmerciful pulsation was much worse than any headache she ever sustained. Misery turned excruciating and she began crying. She didn't think the hurt could get any more intense but it did when the assailant lifted her head off the floor again. Pain burrowed inside her skull and created the impression that her eyeball was palpitating.

WHAM!

Her face smacked the floor once more.

Shei felt and heard the pop in her jawbone. Torment grinded under her ear and gnawed into the gum supporting the top and bottom hind teeth. She didn't believe the impact broke her jaw but it certainly withstood a blow resulting in detrimental damage.

The bitter saltwater taste filled her mouth after the first few teardrops seeped between her lips.

The home intruder lifted her head.

WHAM!

The intense strike was brain jarring and cast her spiraling into a dizzying void of darkness; however, she was a long way from falling unconscious because she still registered unfathomable agony surging throughout her face. She wasn't able to think clearly though, and she had become emotionally numb. Trapped in a semiconscious state of being, Shei could only hope that her violent afflictions would soon conclude - minus having life-threatening results.

WHAM!

Again, her head slammed against the floor.

Being so far out of sorts, she wasn't aware that her head had been picked up. Harsh disorientation seemed to slightly remedy the magnitude of pain. Her mind was someplace distant from body; thoughts became elusive. Borderline absent of having awareness, she felt like she'd been given an epidural. The assailant could ram her head once or twice more on the floor and she probably wouldn't feel a thing because she was past the ability to sense injury. She could be executed on the spot and not be cognizant of her fate.

Shei Rivera was weak, emasculated, insensately damaged...

Entirely unacquainted with how uncertain she was about the duration of her life in the hands of an implicit murderer.

CHAPTER THREE

A sputtering exhaust.

Gasoline.

Motor oil.

Shei immediately recognized such things after becoming cognitively alert. The constant rattle of a faulty exhaust caused the floor to shake beneath her left shoulder. The combined smell of gasoline and motor oil was stout under her nose, and at no point did it lose potency in irritating her eyes and causing them to burn despite being closed.

She didn't know how long she'd been unconscious, and she feared thinking about what more may have happened during whatever length of time after one too many blows to the head knocked her out. She never saw her attacker and wasn't positive the ambush involved just one. Of course, she knew only one person assaulted her but wasn't sure if there might have been a spectator or two standing back and watching events unfold. In fact, she didn't know if she was in the presence of the same asshole that pounced on her.

The outcome of having her head repeatedly smacked against the floor was an aching jaw and explosive headache. She opened her eyes and regardless of being surrounded by darkness all around, the simple act of opening them caused her head to pound more oppressively than any time prior.

Uncomfortably positioned with her knees practically in her chest, Shei stretched her legs out but found they'd go only halfway before she kicked the wall. She realized the confined area was small without seeing it because the back of her head and shoulders pressed the wall behind her.

She wanted to scream with hopes that someone outside would hear her, but she understood that any attempt would amount to a pointless effort since she had what felt like a rag draped across her mouth and tightly knotted on the back of her head. Strangely, this cloth appeared to be the source of those gasoline and motor oil odors unpleasantly inconveniencing her nose and eyes.

Something else she acknowledged was her hands bound against her back and fastened by another article of fabric. Evidently, whoever took the liberty to abduct her had carefully planned the minor details. Then again, maybe she wasn't the first person introduced to the trunk of the vehicle, and every prop implemented in her predicament was integrated based on experience.

Unsure of her destination, Shei feared the worst was yet to come.

A Mazda Convertible drove onto the property of a convenience store and pulled into a parking space in front of the ice coolers alongside a rack of propane tanks - several empty spaces away from a couple of vehicles parked closer to the entrance.

The nicely dressed, clean shaved man that appeared

to be either in his late forties or early fifties stepped out of the driver seat before removing his sunglasses and tossing them through the opening of the rolled down window. He patted the back pocket of his khakis as if checking his wallet and then moved on toward the store.

The alarm system pitched a loud beeping sound when he swung the door open and entered.

"Well look at who in the Sam Hill decided to show their face in these parts," said a tall and burly woman standing by the register behind the counter. "Boy, how long has it been since you've run the streets?"

He stepped away from the door, smiling. "It's been a long while. I don't think I've been down here since I pulled nine months for some bullshit."

She lowered her bifocals to get another look at him. "I was about to say- I think the last time I saw you was close to two years ago. You were running around with that ole Lancaster boy. I remember y'all stopped by here one evening, three sheets to the wind already, and picked up a case of beer because y'all mentioned something about heading to the river."

"Jimmy Lancaster," he said, shaking his head. "Now that is a name that's avoided me lately. Last I heard, he's pulling twenty-five years for that bust he got caught up in. Also, that's an impressive memory you've got there, Dixie. I can't remember shit from yesterday."

Dixie laughed like it was the funniest thing she heard. "Those brain cells have gone through a lot of stress over the years. I'm surprised you're still functioning."

"Yeah. It's been a tough road," he stated, without a hint of jocularity.

His lack of amusement stripped the smile off her face. "If you don't mind me asking, what brings you back to these parts, Elliot?"

He looked across the store and observed the top of its four aisles. A young man paced slowly toward the rear of the second aisle, studying the assemblage of shelved items intently. At the front of the fourth aisle emerged a frail old lady that he didn't notice a minute ago because she was too short to ascend the height of the shelf. She approached the counter, carrying a box of sandwich bags, a pound of flour, and two bottles of MD 20/20. Given her petite frame, Elliot didn't suspect her being a heavy drinker and assumed those two bottles would be enough to knock her on her ass.

The elderly woman and lanky young man were equivalent to the number of vehicles in the parking lot when he arrived. Elliot didn't see anyone else and believed these two were the only customers besides himself.

He glanced at Dixie, who took position behind the register in preparation to tally up the woman's purchases. "I'll get back with you shortly," he stated.

Elliot turned and stepped ahead into the first aisle. He picked up three individually wrapped extra-large beef sticks and didn't care that they all were the same flavor. Then he stepped in front of a variety of chips and fumbled along different brands before picking three bags at random. With too much on his hands already, he went toward the back of the store where a row of soda and cold food coolers lined the wall.

He looked across the top of the shelf and saw the lanky kid frequently glancing at him. "Is there a problem, kiddo?" he asked.

"No," the young man murmured, looking away after making momentary eye contact. "Sorry. I have a habit of seeing who's around me at all times."

Elliot stopped in front of the first cooler of sodas. "You shouldn't stare at everyone you come in contact with, son. Some people don't take too kindly to that sort of thing."

"Yes, sir," the man stated nervously.

Opening the glass door, Elliot reached inside and fetched a bottle of Ginger ale. He turned and glanced at the man that had given him strange looks. Evidently, he heeded the advice because his head didn't raise when Elliot crossed his view on the way to the counter.

Dixie giggled, seeing his choice items. "Now those are an unusual selection. Where's the alcohol?"

He set the items on the counter. "I've probably not had a beer in over a year. Too much shit going on."

She reached under the counter and pulled out a paper bag. Two hard shakes and it opened before she placed it on the counter beside the groceries. "Still dealing like you did back in the day?"

Elliot smiled. "Yes, I am. But I'm very particular with who I deal with these days. You can't really trust people anymore."

"Man, you've got like nine lives. Anybody else would be buried under the jail for all the things you've done," she joked, ringing up the chips.

He scratched his brow. "I've not been very lucky lately. I have some pretty serious charges pending."

"Oh Lord. Now what have you gone and done?" she

inquired.

He arched his shoulders back and sighed. "What have I not done? Let's see; I'm facing possession, trafficking, manufacturing, distribution."

Her jaws dropped. "Jesus, Elliot. That could send you away for a long time. How'd you manage to get a bond?"

"I'm in a unique situation with the Commonwealth," he declared.

She frowned. "Are you snitching?"

"Fuck no, Dixie. You know I wouldn't volunteer any info to the po-po," he quickly retaliated.

"I didn't take you for the type," she admitted, sliding all the beef sticks down inside the bag.

He went for his wallet. "There's a particular stipulation that has potential to get me off the hook. It's all legal politics. You know how the system loves to operate."

She took his debit card when offered and swiped it through the reader. "Does any of that have to do with why you're back in the area?"

He grinned and retrieved the card from her after the payment cleared. "I'm a shady man. Can't be entertaining you with all of my business affairs. But I am here to do a job. A quick in and out, basically."

She slid the bag to the front of the counter. "Just don't get yourself into any more trouble."

He snatched the bag and lowered it by his side. "Ya know, I'm going to take those words to heart. I've got to do what I'm here to do, and I'm disappearing after that - dropping off the face of the earth."

"I hope you still decide to drop in and see me every

once in a while," she said.

He winked. "I'll make it a priority. It's been a pleasure seeing you for the first time in a long while. Take good care of yourself, Dixie."

The ride turned from smooth to bumpy.

Shei could not lay in peace for one second. The back of her head kept hitting the wall, preventing any hopeful opportunity for the immensity of her headache to decrease. Whatever rough terrain also jerked her back and forth constantly. All aching parts of her body reminded her just how physically traumatized they truly were, which briefly flashed her back to relive the experience of getting smothered while her face was bashed against the floor.

She didn't know the amount of time she'd been riding in this small compartment but it indisputably felt long enough to place her so far from home that she would have no sense of direction if she got loose and fled her abductor. Thinking about the feel of the path beneath her, Shei believed she was on the trail toward an absence of society.

If she miraculously found a way to remove the rag from covering her mouth, then it would do her no good because nobody would hear her scream.

Her gut feeling gave the strong impression that wherever she was being taken, she'd be just as well to have law enforcement officially presume her dead.

The dominant horror - most petrifying to acknowledge - pertained to the contingency that this morning could be the last time she saw Sierra.

CHAPTER FOUR

An assortment of clutter overlaid most of the visually expensive wooden office desk. A stack of documentation in an open manila file folder served as the centerpiece. Both sides of the folder contained an equal amount of paper. Pages on the left were situated facedown, and those on the right were positioned upright with a body of text embossing the top page. In various sections of the top few paragraphs were words of particular importance highlighted within yellow blocks.

Liam Rivera leaned forward in his oversized brown leather office chair and analyzed the documentation closely. One hand gripped the wide handle of a half full coffee mug, and the other held the yellow highlighter awaiting action for when he stumbled upon another word needing pinpointed for a later date. After reading through the remainder of information on the page, he laid it over facedown on the left side and began to examine the next.

He got three sentences into reading and then stopped and highlighted four words. Before proceeding with another sentence, he lifted the mug and took a nice long sip of stout coffee. No sugar. No creamer. Straight up face wrenching bitterness.

He set the mug down and returned to studying the document.

Seconds after he picked up reading, two unexpected knocks breached the office door.

He looked up and saw it open without allowing him time to verbally recognize someone on the other side requesting his attention. Two familiar individuals entered the room, and who they were immediately puzzled him about why they had come to see him. The second man shut the door and the two uniformed men walked in front of their state attorney's desk.

"Gentleman," Liam said, retiring the highlighter pen on his unfinished studies of legal documentation. "To what do we owe the pleasure?"

"I'm afraid we have some unfortunate news," said the first officer.

"Sheriff Peterson, what can possibly be so bothersome at the start of this fine morning?" Liam asked, tugging the buttoned cuffs on his long sleeve shirt prior to placing his elbows on the desk and bringing both hands together to rest underneath his chin.

"I don't know a better way to say this. This morning we received a call from the Brier Orchard cul de sac. One of your daughter's neighbors reported seeing a man drag her across the back lawn and into the thicket leading to Denton Drive. The witness claims that Shei appeared unresponsive because she wasn't fighting back in any way. Our caller didn't get a good look at the suspect but we're going to do everything in our power to get the best composite sketch possible," said Sheriff Peterson.

Liam frowned and flung his hands out from under his chin before striking them upon the desk. "That's impossible. I just spoke with her this morning after she dropped my granddaughter off at school. It wasn't all that long ago."

"I know none of this sounds plausible, sir, but we responded to the call as soon as it came in and what we-"

"Did you go to her residence?" Liam interrupted.

The officer accompanying Sheriff Peterson nodded and adjusted his tactical belt. "That's what I was getting to, sir. We went to her property and did discover her vehicle on the premises; however, your daughter was not home and we found no sign of a struggle. I don't like to admit it but this is shaping up to resemble a classic textbook abduction."

Liam leaned back in his chair. "That's a ridiculous assumption. Shei has never involved herself with anyone who would want to hurt her. She has very high standards for herself and doesn't trust just anybody."

"We're actually looking at the situation from a different angle, sir. None of this may involve anyone she knows," said the officer.

"What are you getting at?" Liam questioned.

"Your daughter doesn't have a significant other or any love interests, correct?" the policeman inquired.

"No. Not that I'm aware," Liam reacted. He looked at the framed photograph peering at him from the back right corner of the desk. The picture exhibited a happy family. A slightly younger version of himself (noticeable by the minimal gray in his hair), Shei in her late teens, and his darling wife Sheba.

"Sierra's father is a legit piece of shit but I do not believe that he'd go to any extreme lengths to hurt Shei. Honestly, he has no reason to because he's got nothing to do with his own daughter. As far as any other man is concerned, Shei kind of shut down after her mother passed. She didn't trust herself to let someone else get close to her after losing her mother and seeing the relationship with Sierra's father go sour. She fears getting attached to someone and then suffering loss all over again. So I can't think of anybody that would be out to hurt her," he stated.

"Liam, I think what Officer Abhrams is trying to say is you're one of the top prosecuting attorney's in the state. The best in all of Southwest Virginia. You've taken on some nasty defendants in many high profile cases. Roanoke is swarming with people that have paid for their guilt based on your burden of proof. We're thinking that whoever broke into Shei's home might be someone you have gone up against in the courtroom," Sheriff Peterson aired out.

"Or quite possibly someone involved in a pending case," Officer Abhrams added.

Liam crossed his arms on his chest and strained his brows at Sheriff Peterson. "So you're saying someone took my child with intent to get back at me for doing what is lawfully necessary to make certain that our future generations grow up in a safe community?"

Sheriff Peterson nodded. "That is exactly what we believe. It is the only scenario we have found to be logical. The only issue is investigating all of your past cases, beginning with the most recent, and trying to find which ones involve individuals with the most extensive records. The only problem with this is that you've had thousands of cases."

Liam's face squinched. "Nineteen years worth."

Officer Abhrams sighed. "It's going to make our job

extremely difficult but we're going to try our damndest to catch a lead."

Liam raised one hand to his face and swiped the side of a finger across his stubbly chin. "You said that your eyewitness didn't get a good look at this perp?"

"Unfortunately, no. We're going to attempt building a profile based on what little information they are able to provide us. Other than that, all I know to do is talk to people on Denton Drive to see if anybody saw anything," Sheriff Peterson answered.

Liam grunted. "You guys do that. Touch base with me no matter how minor the details. I want to be informed at all times when new information comes in."

"You've got it," Sheriff Peterson replied.

"We'll be in touch, sir, as soon as we've got something," Officer Abhrams mentioned.

The officers stepped away from the desk.

Liam listened for the door to close before callously slapping the desktop and then looking at the immortalized portrait of the perfect family again. He admired Sheba, reflecting on how she was the heart of the family - always making sure nothing ripped them apart. Then he glanced at Shei. Her good manners and tenderheartedness seemed to have existed forever ago. He missed this polite child, unscathed by deplorable leeches she would grow to have relationships with and eventually a kid. Nowadays, he and Shei were lucky to get along and agree on whatever topic for one day. The lone thread holding them together was Sierra. That little girl meant the world to him, even on those rare days when he felt the only family that genuinely loved him had taken such adoration to the grave.

He couldn't overlook how much Shei changed since her mother's passing.

As far as Liam was concerned, he lost his true daughter four years ago.

CHAPTER FIVE

Elliot brought the Convertible to a stop at the broad dead end of a gravel driveway in the middle of nowhere. Forestland stretched for miles, from one mountain on to the next. In front of the driveway stood an elegant two-story cabin. With a wrap-around porch, huge patio for hosting cookouts, and what appeared to be three large tinted windows laid in the roof facing the driveway, the property was beyond anything one might expect to stumble across so deep in the boonies.

He picked up the paper bag from the passenger seat and honked the horn once before exiting the vehicle. This time he didn't remove the sunglasses and fling them into the car. Instead, he kept them on and admired the retreat to prevent whatever occupant(s) from noticing how closely he was paying attention. Walking backwards toward the rear of the vehicle, Elliot did not take his eyes off the property.

The cabin door opened.

A lone man stepped out onto the porch. Not much about his face could be distinguished beneath the curved bill of the baseball cap pulled over his eyes. The only feature Elliot could identify was his dark facial hair. His short boxed beard was well groomed with the same standard applied to the hair around his mouth and across his chin. He was charmingly suited to the atmosphere; square toe work boots, denim jeans, black and gray long-sleeve plaid shirt. If he was aiming to give the impression that he was one true southern gent, then he nailed it nicely on appearance.

"Casper Melhourne?!" Elliot called out, standing alongside the rear fender.

The cabin dweller didn't answer by the name. In fact, he didn't say anything. Alternatively, he took a few steps forward, paused, and then began to make his way down the steep flight of steps. He touched the ground and proceeded in the direction of the vehicle. Not once did he look up to get a better view of Elliot.

"You forget your name, or are you just hard of hearing?" Elliot inquired.

The man stopped at an arm's length distance in front of him. He smirked below the bill of his hat. Then his head drifted back, erasing the majority of shadow that masked him like some fugitive bandit. Those eyes - predominantly green with an odd hint of gray - pierced Elliot on account of their peculiar radiance. There was something about them that Elliot could not quite perceive. He didn't know if it was something singularly offsetting or involved a combination of triggers. The one thing he did take away from noticing them was that things somehow turned intense - quick.

"I find it impolite to yell just to be heard. We may be out here in the jungle of the Blue Ridge Mountains but it doesn't mean we can't speak to each other like grown ass men," the bearded man addressed, nudging the bill of his hat higher off his face. "But to answer your question, yeah, I'm Casper."

Elliot chuckled. "You ain't gotta try convincing me you're a model citizen. I know your backstory, and we're in this for the same cause."

"You don't know shit about me," Casper spluttered.

Elliot stepped around the back of the vehicle. "I know you're looking to score the same bullshit deal that I am. Guess that makes us partners until all of this blows over."

"I'm not your partner," Casper replied.

Elliot tossed the bag at him. Fortunately, the top was folded over and rolled down so many times that it didn't unravel and lose all its contents. "There! Take that. It's just enough to get through these few days."

Casper caught the bag with one hand. "What is this?"

"Chips and shit. Wouldn't want to see anyone starve," Elliot announced, lifting the car keys looped around his finger and jingling them briefly. "Sure you don't want to swap me places?"

Casper refrained showing enjoyment in having him company. He didn't smile, and he obviously wasn't there to shoot the shit. "Come on with it, man. We ain't got all day."

"Settle down. No need to go and get all anxious," Elliot replied, unlocking the trunk.

The door raised and uncovered a sight that brought Elliot to smile immediately. Shei Rivera lay practically doubled over in the small compartment. Arms and mouth bound, she was completely hopeless and only able to look up at her merciless attacker admiring her as if she was some cherished prize. Hair disheveled, cheeks reddened as the result of constant crying, and one side of her face succumbed to dark bruising already, she was not the same high spirited young lady that had jammed and sang along to her favorite tune earlier.

Elliot waved at her in a way of wiggling his fingers individually. "Hello, again. Sorry if I got a little too rough with you. Picking people up isn't ordinarily my line of work."

She groaned behind the cloth.

He laughed at the melody of misery subdued. "Don't voice your concerns to me. I'm just the middle man."

"Christ, man. Would you get her out already?" Casper asked.

Elliot reached inside and grabbed behind the top of her arm but hesitated doing anything with her and glanced at his accomplice. "Someone sounds like they're in a hurry to have this one all to themself."

Attempting to snap the tension out of his neck, Casper cocked his head to one side and then the other. "That's not it. Fact of the matter is I didn't sign on to do this just to stand out here and play *let's get personal*. I've got a job to do and I intend to do it. Now would you please escort her from the vehicle so that I can uphold my end of the bargain?"

Elliot slipped the tip of his tongue between his lips and strained his neck muscles momentarily. "Thin on patience, are we?"

Casper sniffed deeply before firing a loogie off to the side. "What got me here killed my patience a long time ago."

Elliot pulled Shei from the compartment and stood

her upright. Her legs were a little shaky and she swayed a couple of times; eventually, she got used to being on her feet again and steadily grounded herself. The one thing she hadn't readjusted to after being stowed in the trunk was the blaring sunlight. It was a total calamity on her eyes and she bowed her head to prevent observing her primary assailant since she couldn't view him clearly anyway.

He grabbed her hips and jolted his own to one side - performing some kind of bizarre dance ritual in celebration of tagging the perfect game. "Woowee!" he boasted, jerking her forward and grinding himself against her. "I just might have to stick around awhile. Plenty of meat here for the both of us."

Burying her face on his confidently protruding chest, Shei wriggled in his vigorous grip but was too weak and panicky to gain an inch of distance.

Elliot must have instinctively recognized her discomfort because he made sure to increase humiliation by reaching behind with one hand and playfully groping her ass.

"Would you prefer that I look after you, pretty little thing?" he whispered down to her.

Shei didn't answer. She didn't offer to lean back and look at him. She did only what was natural for a woman in her position - which was cry, sniffle, and inhale the nauseating fumes absorbed in the rag. Although she did fear that her safety was in jeopardy, Shei clinged to the hope that one of these men was more lenient than the other and whatever harm destined for her would be minimally produced. If she was ordained to receive a portentous fate, then she hoped that any anguish associated would influence a swift outcome.

"Listen, man. I don't know what your deal is or what you've got to prove, but acting out with some bullshit isn't going to get either of us anywhere. We've got an opportunity to set things straight and I don't need you fucking up my end," Casper enunciated, playing voyeur to the indecency.

Elliot jiggled the handful of ass cheek in its white midthigh skater skirt before releasing and giving it one hard slap. Shei squealed and her entire body jerked following the unexpected strike on her bosom.

He laughed. "It's a shame knowing this ain't nothing but waste material."

Then he glanced at Casper, narrowing his eyes. "Don't you fall in love with this fine thing. The boss man probably wouldn't be inclined to forgive, if you were to go and invest in self pleasure."

Casper lowered his head and dragged one boot back through the gravel. "You don't see me grabbing ass and salivating. I know my responsibility, and unlike you, I've got the virtue to see it through."

"You saying I ain't got the right mind for the job?" Elliot snapped straightaway.

"I think you've got an issue-"

"Look!" Elliot squalled. He pushed her away and then spun her around assertively. Reaching under the front of her face, he yanked her head sideways to show off the badly beaten side. "The only issue I've got is that she's still breathing. I could have done the job by now and avoided putting us in this mess. But then, you wouldn't play a role in this if that was the case. I'd be in the clear on all my shit and never have to worry again about people meddling in my interests. But no - as my luck would have it, someone else's shit crosses mine."

Casper surveyed the trauma bestowed on her face. His thoughts suddenly took him back to childhood and on a night when one of his single mother's drunk and drugged boyfriends plowed his bare knuckle fist into her face, bloodying her lip and knocking out the top two front teeth. She always expressed a fondness for the roughneck breed of man and there was never a relationship that didn't involve her getting a beatdown, but this particular memory stayed with him like a gaping wound oozing infection while refusing to heal. Inspecting Shei's voluminous contusion advertised to him what type of man Elliot was honestly. The kind of man that lacked morality. Actually, Elliot wasn't the sort of individual he'd define as being a man. This guy was scum. A genuine bottomfeeder. Regardless if she was the very essence of a scurvy stratagem, Casper didn't believe she was deserving of such inhumane treatment.

He pulled the whole tongue in cheek, preventing himself from rattling off his opinion on the matter. "What the fuck happened to her?"

Elliot rubbed the back of his hand down the battered side of her face, and she flinched when he did. Perhaps she felt pain with even the most gentle touch.

He sighed and winked at Casper. "Sometimes you hit a little bump when business is flowing. She let her head get in the way of things but it wasn't anything I couldn't handle in the end. As you can tell, she overcame it with no problem."

Personally, Casper didn't care to hear what Elliot had to say. There was no respect for a sleazebag that resorted to committing violence against women, and listening to the bastard jokingly brag about assaulting her went a long way in rankling him. One of his knees gave out but not because of sudden weakness. The strength in his leg collapsed because his subconscious self was ready to pounce forward and concede Elliot to an ass whipping he'd never forget. Casper wanted to literally beat him within an inch of his life but didn't react because there was too much at stake. He had his own expectations for when all of this came to a close and turning on his brethren would only cause complications and potentially annihilate his triumph of becoming set free from past convictions. Tolerating Elliot for the eventual positive outcome was far better than bursting out with pure hatred surging through him right now.

"What's the story, she fell down - bumped her head?" Casper asked, deescalating his awareness of the situation to prevent enticing a confrontation.

Elliot sighed. "We ain't got to get into all that backstory. Besides, it's irrelevant given what's to come. All that matters is she's here now. I did my part and the rest is yours."

"Okay," Casper replied, nodding once. "Then I guess we're finished here. You've got a life to get back to, I'm sure. Now I've got to follow through on my duties."

"Ya know-" Elliot crossed one arm against Shei's chest and pinned her to him before sneaking the other one down onto the bottom of her skirt. He began to raise it slowly, feeling her tremble constantly while listening to her whimper all the while. The skirt lifted above the most personal region of her body to show lace ocean blue panties. He moved his hand from her chest and creeped down her body. Stretching beyond his other hand holding the skirt against her stomach, Elliot widened his hand against the delicate fabric between her legs. He rubbed up and down again. With Shei having no concept about what might happen next, he halted scraping between her thighs and grabbed a handful of crotch. She squirmed instantly but could do nothing more.

"I could've easily had my way with this one. She's such a fine piece of work that the thought was tempting, but I figured it wouldn't be wise to get sidetracked while doing business. For you, on the other hand, it's a different story. You've got to stare at this thing for the next few nights; might ought to try it out," he added.

Irritated by his behavior prior to this latest stunt, Casper looked away to avoid seeing her intimate area partly exposed. He unintentionally glimpsed into the Convertible's backseat and recognized Elliot was traveling with a high powered McMillan TAC 50 assault rifle. This style of weapon was popularized on the battlefield; Casper got the impression that Elliot was not carrying it for sport.

"Let her go, man. She's gone through enough," Casper urged, still refusing to feast his eyes on her inner thighs.

"Hold a damn minute," Ellios said, letting go of her crotch and allowing the skirt to drop before he returned both hands on her hips. "You're going to back out of the job, aren't you?"

"Dammit, man - no!" Casper replied.

"You ain't acting right," Elliot stated.

"What the hell is that supposed to mean?" Casper asked.

"You're being a little too proper for a couple of grown ass men with a sweet piece of pussy out in the middle of absolutely fucking nowhere. You act like this bitch is somebody. She ain't nothing," Elliot declared.

Casper looked at them now that she wasn't improperly advertised. "How I conduct myself has nothing to do with my job performance. She's a female, big deal. I've dealt with my fair share that were exactly like her."

Elliot shoved her the short distance and she crashed into Casper without budging him slightly. She didn't look up to view the identity of her second captor, and she didn't attempt to stop him from taking a firm grip of her either. Instead, she caved entirely in his hold as though the inability to escape was formerly perceived.

"All right, Mister Playboy. I think I've got you pegged. You're the type of guy - natural charmer - with the God-given resources to sweep any woman you lay eyes on off her feet. There are none beyond reach for a man like you. Women are drawn for whatever reason. Then you boast about all those fine asses to guys like me, who these women view as pathetic sloths and avoid getting to know," Elliot mentioned.

"Actually, I don't consider myself-"

Elliot slammed the trunk door shut. "I hope every second in the remaining hours of her life are the most tormenting moments she's ever felt! Fuck this privileged bitch! And fuck you too!" he shrieked.

Casper put one hand in front of him, signaling Elliot

to stand down. "Chill out, man. I don't know what shit you're on but it's got you delusional. Ain't nobody categorizing anybody. We're here for the same reason. Which is to set shit straight."

Elliot brushed both hands through his hair and then brought the back of one against his mouth. "God, what I would give to see the outcome of this."

"I'll take care of it," Casper assured.

Elliot stepped forward but then stopped just inches away from Casper's hand touching his chest. His wild eyes gazed deeply into his accomplice's state of uncertainty. "Do us both a favor and end it slowly. Let her feel what entitlement really has to offer. As a bonus, you can carve my fucking initials in her flesh. Just make damn certain I'm one of the last few people that cross her mind. If not, then you and I will cross paths long after this is over."

CHAPTER SIX

Liam Rivera anxiously blasted through the door without knocking.

Inside the room sat a well-tailored, gray haired man at a disarranged desk of his own. Inscribed on a golden placard facing two chairs in front of the desk were the words *Honorable Alfonso Reyes*. Liam assumed that he must have been working on his computer because he jerked away from the keyboard and slouched back in his chair before toying with his tie.

Liam never took his eyes off him while closing the door. "Alfonso, we've got a little bit of an issue."

"What the fuck are you doing barging in my office like this? If the wrong person saw you just now, then it's liable to get around we're discussing indictments. I don't need rumors getting spread that there's some shady shit taking place in my courtroom," Alfonso voiced sternly.

"Indictments can go to hell right now. They're the furthest thing from my mind. Shei was picked up from her home this morning," Liam mentioned.

"This has resulted in a situation how? Did you not arrange for her to partake in a private business excursion?" Alfonso inquired, keeping the same rigorous tone.

"I did, but there has been an unexpected consequence," Liam claimed.

Alfonso frowned. "What did you fuck up?"

"It's nothing to do with fucking up anything. A man was spotted dragging her away from the house. One of her neighbors reported it to authorities. Sheriff Peterson has been here and spoke with me about it already," Liam stated.

Alfonso shook his head and made multiple quiet clicking sounds with his tongue somehow. "Yes, goddammit. You have gone and fucked up. Do you realize how heavily involved I am in this? My reputation is on the line. My retirement."

Liam approached the desk. "We've worked together for sixteen years now. I've never done anything to throw shade your way, and I'm not about to let it happen this time. I'll take care of it. You've got my word."

"*Got your word.* What good is that going to do me? Some asshole was seen hauling your daughter off," Alfonso griped.

"The caller didn't get a clear view of him. Sheriff Peterson and his boys don't know where to begin looking. Nothing is in jeopardy," Liam assured.

Reaching down, Alfonso opened the bottom right hand desk drawer and pulled out a half bottle of Tequila. He unfastened the lid and turned it up to his mouth, downing a few hard gulps. Shortly afterward, he withdrew the bottle and gasped before fastening the lid and returning the beverage inside the drawer.

"You'd better straighten this mess out, and I mean now. I'm not going to have the Sheriff snoop around and ask questions. I play too large of a role and will not allow any risks," he said.

"Everything is scheduled to still go like originally

planned. We've got a reliable person tying up all of our loose ends. There is not going to be a trail leading back to anywhere. Trust me on this," Liam stated.

"I'm trusting you to fix it right now. Fix it and get the hell out of here. The longer you stick around, the more those clerks out there are going to suspect we're in cahoots over something," Alfonso snapped.

"All right. I'll tell you what I'll do," Liam said, frantically digging inside his pants pocket and retrieving his mobile phone. "I'll send him a message to be at my house this evening for dinner. I'll go over the details and make myself very clear that not a single trace is to be left behind. My granddaughter will be the only other person there but she'll not have a clue about what's going on."

"This cleaner that you've hired, how do you know he isn't going to back out?" Alfonso inquired.

"Because he's got pending charges that he wants erased. If not, then he's looking to go away for a good while. I may have also offered fifteen grand," Liam admitted, speedily striking the letters on his phone's keyboard. "That's it - it's done! Nothing more for you to sit there and stress about."

"And if he doesn't show?" Alfonso asked curiously.

"He's going to. There's too much at stake for him to turn his back on me," Liam replied, sliding the phone into his pocket.

Alfonso sighed and spun the chair sideways to face the window overlooking the courtyard. His worrying eyes scanned from one side of the window to the other as their corner wrinkles thickened and deepened with his overwrought squint.

"I'm not sure how I feel about this. I don't know why I let you talk me into it to begin with," he mentioned.

Seemingly negligent of the judge's concern, Liam smiled and calmly reminded him, "A hundred thousand can convince a man to do things he wouldn't normally subject himself to. You've been eyeing and talking about retirement for quite some time, now you can comfortably own it."

Alfonso shook his head. "I just feel that I'm not doing right in Dillon's name."

"If he was here, then he would be understanding of the situation. He'd be happy to see you finally have the opportunity to get out of this place," Liam fired back quickly.

Obviously, Alfonso had nothing more to say on the matter since he remained quiet.

His departure from the conversation didn't prevent Liam from reinforcing positivity. "Next week this will all be water under the bridge. You're retiring. I'm retiring. Individuals are having their history cleansed. It's a win no matter how you look at it. So rest easy. We will not have any issues arise."

CHAPTER SEVEN

Soon after Elliot hauled ass down the road, kicking up a dense trail of gray gravel dust, Casper escorted Shei inside the cabin. He sort of proved himself less savage than his counterpart by opening the door and allowing her to proceed ahead of him. Shei entered cautiously. She didn't know what to expect anymore. Physical abuse was not something named in her agreement, but it happened. Also, she wasn't informed that she'd be suffocated. The man was supposed to politely pick her up at home, hide her inside the trunk of his vehicle, and deliver her under the pretense that it was a legitimate abduction. However, everything he did to her was real - which made her very fearful of what this man might do.

She looked around the large open space. The fireplace was constructed from rock cemented together, and centered on the overmantle high above the vacant firebox was a sixteen-point deer head mounted on a wooden plaque. Laying across the hardwood floor in front of the fireplace was a large animal hide. She didn't know the type of animal exactly but assumed it was bearskin. At the center of the room was an oversized black leather couch with matching loveseat and recliner on either side. In front of the couch stood a long glass top coffee table, and on it were a few books and expensive tile drink coasters. Affixed to the strip of log wall between two huge windows across from the furniture was a massive 75-inch flatscreen television.

Behind the couch was a large and luxurious kitchen island, separating the living room and galley. Four tall stools lined across the front and Shei could only guess that there were four more on the backside. Since the place lacked a dining table for guests to have dinner, she supposed this was the alternative. Beyond the island was a stainless steel double-stack oven built into the log wall, and not far from it stood a refrigerator of the same make.

She looked up toward the A-frame roof since the living room was a spacious area with no ceiling. The kitchen was the only place with a ceiling but above the island she recognized a bannister running crossways. On the opposite side was a narrow walkway and wall with two doors widely spaced out from each other. She didn't see a staircase leading to the second floor but imagined that it couldn't be too far out of view.

The place as a whole was incredible. If Casper owned it, then he definitely had the cash flow to invest in making it a dreamscape.

Casper approached behind her after shutting the door and arranged the paper bag between his legs before reaching up and unfastening the knot on the back of her head. He pulled the rag away and she gasped. Finally, Shei was able to breathe and not inhale those toxic fumes. In a sense, having the cloth removed brought instant relief. Despite now being capable of voicing her concerns or opinions for that matter, she didn't attempt to mutter one word. Extremely afraid of what he might try to do, she didn't want to strive to say anything potentially threatening to her safety.

He reached on her back and unbound her hands. Shei didn't know what to think about this fragmental release from captivity. She raised her hands in front of her and circled her fingers around one wrist while discomfort from being tied lingered.

"You can relax now. I'm not going to hurt you," he said, tossing the two fabrics behind him on the floor beside the door.

Shei still refused to speak. She had endured enough in such little time to traumatize a person for life. Besides the violent abduction, she was inappropriately assaulted by having a man's hand grope between her legs. Nothing in her mind suspected things were going to be okay. For all she knew, Casper might have it planned to rape her; even worse, he could have a grave out in the middle of nowhere waiting for her already. While the original blueprint intended for her to strike, everything she encountered up to this point revealed the agenda she thought she knew was obsolete.

Casper pulled the brown bag from between his legs and pressed the other hand flat against her lower back, nudging forward. She didn't know where he wanted her to go but she shuffled onward anyway.

"Take a seat on one of those stools," he requested, keeping his hand on her as they advanced past the leather furniture. "I'll make you an ice pack. The least it will do is relieve some of that swelling."

Shei pulled the last stool on the left out from under the edge of the island countertop and sat down slowly. He maneuvered around the other side and continued toward the narrow door next to the double-stack oven. He opened the door and inside the small space stood a five-gallon garbage can. Without opening the bag given to him by Elliot, he tossed it in the trash.

"I wouldn't give you anything he purchased. Not after all that he's done," he said, closing the door and then scampering across to the overhead cabinets above the stainless steel stovetop and adjacent sink.

She watched him ransack the first cabinet as if he had no idea where the item in mind was located. He moved on to the next cabinet and did the same. When reaching the third one, he shuffled through a few items before removing a box of ziploc freezer bags. He withdrew one bag and threw the box in the cabinet.

"I don't appreciate what that ole boy did to you. You're not big enough to harm a flea," he mentioned, stepping to the refrigerator. "If we'd been at the bar or in any other sort of scenario, I would have whipped his ass. But being out here, a man's really got to watch himself. There's no telling what goes through the mind of a feller like him. Say the wrong thing and they're liable to go off the deep end on you."

The double door fridge was half freezer with a built-in ice dispenser. He opened the bag, situated it under the dispenser, and pushed the eject button. The sound of ice blasting out of the chute was loud but the commotion was only temporary since the bag filled in a few seconds. He pulled it out, shook it a couple of times to even out the ice, and sealed the ziplock.

Instead of handing her the bag in its raw plastic

form, Casper opened the top drawer next to the sink and grabbed a washcloth. He wrapped the bag twice and folded the loose ends so that the rag would stay in place when applied to her face. Then he stepped in front of her sitting across from him and reached out the ice pack for her to take.

"It's not the best but it serves the purpose," he said.

Reluctant to accept his offer, she stared at the good deed hovering in front of her.

"Go ahead," he insisted, pushing it closer toward her. "You're going to have to get accustomed to being treated respectfully regardless of the predicament. I'm not some chauvinistic asshole who's going to bash you based on the misconception that your life is of lesser value."

Shei stayed silent but did take the ice pack. She looked over the right side of the kitchen and through the window, recognizing a thicket of trees beside the cabin and past them she saw one mountaintop beyond another, beyond another. Acknowledging the idea that she was off the grid of civilization, she turned and touched the ice pack on her face before lowering her head and staring at the countertop to avoid making contact with him.

"Where are we?" she whispered.

"Apple Orchard Mountain, I believe. The only thing I know for sure is we're in Botetourt County," he replied.

"Is this your place?" she asked.

"Umm… No," he intoned. "I was brought here yesterday evening. I'm kind of in the same situation you are - except I'm on the opposite side of the fence. The job I was given relates to you. We're not going to get into that mess right now though, because you wouldn't believe everything I told you anyway. First we've got to show that we can trust each other before we jump into discussing that complicated matter."

Shei opened her mouth as wide as it could stretch and closed it again. Surprisingly, she felt the ice pack went a long way in soothing her pain. Before turning numb, her jaw throbbed intensely any time she moved her lips.

"Trust. That's an awful powerful word to be throwing around. There's just one problem. I've had a bag put over my head, my face bounced off the floor, kidnapped, and sexually violated all in one morning. Trusting someone is the furthest thing from my mind. It just isn't going to happen," she made clear.

He grinned. "Then we'll start with dinner. Do you like steak? Scalloped potatoes? There is plenty of food to get us through these next few days. I can definitely fix you something better than bullshit chips and whatever else was in that bag."

She removed the ice pack. "Based on your reason for being here, what's supposed to happen after a few days? I know what I was told but I want to hear yours."

Casper took off his hat and laid it in front of him on the counter. "We'll get into that but not at the moment. It'll make for some good conversation over dinner."

Eventually, she looked at him and did not pull away. She felt that she couldn't stray from looking at him even if she wanted to withdraw. Shei had no idea the peculiar nature of his eyes possessed an uncertain effect on Elliot; however, she was suddenly now experiencing a similar result. He somehow naturally overcame her trepidation by peering in her eyes. She succumbed to an array of things;

serenity, consolation, and an unusual attraction that - if under ordinary circumstances - might have caused her to feel smitten over him. She couldn't pretend he wasn't handsome and she most certainly could not ignore how just his presence contributed intensively to her interests, but she did have control over not making these qualities apparent. It had been a long time since she viewed a man as eye candy, and so she couldn't let this pleasant sight get in the way of conflict, especially for the reason that she didn't really know anything about him personally.

"How's that face feeling?" he inquired.

She glanced at his ballcap, breaking their momentary direct contact. "It's okay. The ice did take most of the ache away. Thank you."

"Good. I ran across some Tylenol when I was snooping last night. I'll give you a few after you shower. They should help keep the pain to a minimum throughout the night," he said.

"Shower?" she asked quickly.

Casper laughed. "Yes, ma'am. You've got the shit beat out of you and was locked in the back of a vehicle. I'm not sure if you notice, but you reek of gasoline and oil. The shit is probably absorbed in your skin. Anyway, a shower will not only have you smelling good but it will also help to make you feel better. Maybe it'll help ease your mind too. It's the most I can do before we start getting acquainted with each other a little better. I told you that I'm not going to hurt you in any way. You've got to trust me a bit at some point."

She waved her hand in refusal. "Nah. I'm good, really. I took a shower just a few hours ago. I don't actually feel dirty, and I'm okay mentally. I appreciate your willingness to help though."

"Nonsense," he retaliated, standing from the stool and easing toward her around the side of the island. "If I think something will make you feel better, then that's the direction we're going. I'm not trying to sound like a prick. I just know your mind is likely scattered in a hundred different places at once that you don't know what might be the right thing to do. I'm only trying to help."

"You don't know me," she fired back calmly. "And I don't need anyone's help."

He took the ice pack from her and placed it out of reach on the side of the counter where he'd been sitting. "Be easy, little lady. There is no reason to get defensive. I'm simply being nice and doing whatever I can to help."

Although Shei didn't feel completely uncomfortable by his behavior, she felt that she'd been put on edge because of its sudden strangeness. Her guard was up. The last man that demanded her to do things was Sierra's father, and he was severely abusive in how he handled those occasions. Casper might be dealing with her in the nicest way possible but her PTSD was viewing the situation differently. She was concerned that he may have the potential to snap at her during any moment.

He grasped both of her hands and guided her off the stool gently. She believed her only choice was to cooperate and eliminate the likelihood of him lashing out unexpectedly. He ushered her across the left side of the kitchen and through an average size doorway leading into an extremely short hallway. Upon entering, she recognized an opening on the left and inside of it was a set of stairs going upward. She assumed they accessed the second floor since she didn't notice any other way. The hallway ended almost immediately past the opening to the staircase and in front of her stood a door.

"Go ahead," he insisted.

Not wanting to disobey and risk making him angry, she reached ahead and opened the door. What she discovered on the other side was a large bathroom, materialistically enriched like all of the other areas she'd seen so far. Directly across the room in front of her stood a walk in shower with a beautiful smoke stained glass front encasement. On the left side of the room was a long countertop, stretching from behind the door and over to the wall behind the shower. Mounted inside the counter were two separate sinks. On the edge of the counter nearest the shower was a white towel folded neatly, and next to it were gray and white articles of clothing - both were also folded nicely with white on top of gray. She wasn't one-hundred percent sure but she suspected they were meant for her to put on after the shower that he was adamant about her taking. Lastly, she marveled silently over the enormous mirror spanning the height and width of the portion of wall above the counter.

The right side of the room was bare in comparison to everything she witnessed up to now. The toilet was mounted in front of the furthest wall, and several feet in front of it stood an exterior double door storage container.

Shei crept inside the room and attempted to shut the door-

But it wouldn't budge.

She turned and noticed Casper standing in the

doorway. One leg pressed against the door while his large boot rested firmly alongside the bottom center. She looked at him strangely, confused about what his ulterior motive might be for blocking her from closing it.

He smiled at her awkwardly. "This stays open."

She gnarled her lips at his remark. "Excuse me, but I'm about to do as you requested and take a shower. Which means you can't watch."

He chuckled. "Just because it's open doesn't mean I'm going to look at you. I've seen a decent number of naked women in my life, so you're nothing new."

"You think I'm unattractive?" she questioned straightaway.

He looked down at her body, taking in the view one inch at a time before looking up again. "No. That's not what I'm saying. The point I'm trying to make is that I'll let you do what you need to do and be respectful about it, but we are going to have to be in sight of each other at all times. That way we both can prove that one isn't trying to pull something over on the other."

"I don't necessarily need to do anything," she said shortly.

"Come on," he said, tilting his head to one side. "We've got no reason to not get along."

Shei could only look at him with disbelief. She didn't know where to begin disagreeing but thought of multiple reasons off the top of her head about why they shouldn't coddle each other with generosity. Either Casper didn't take the tension between them seriously, or he was exorbitantly narrow minded. The lack of benignancy in his expression insinuated that he was pathetically out of touch with reality.

He scooted his foot away from pressing the door and took a step back. "Are we on the same page?"

She didn't bother to say anything and shut the door in his face.

"Dammit," he griped, raising his fist at the door.

Maybe the plan was to ram his hand against it, but he didn't. He thought of what the ramifications might consist; she positively would not trust him if he acted out with frustration, and the distance between them may increase to become irresolvable. Taking no initiative to escalate the stress amongst them, he unclenched his fist and lowered from what could have transpired to be a frantic attack on the door. Then he took a deep breath and opened it.

She stalled immediately and whirled around - eyeing him tyrannically - while standing within reach of the smoke gray enclosure. "Really?! I can't get ten minutes to myself?"

"A lot can happen in ten minutes," he replied.

She flung her arms up and away from her sides. "Look around. What could possibly happen?"

He smirked. "Anything. You could get shampoo in your eyes. That would burn and you'd not be able to see your way around. Know what would happen? You'd call for me to come running and hand you that towel to dab your face."

"I doubt I'd need you to come to the rescue," she said, turning her back to him and opening the door on the enclosure. "Are you going to stand there the entire time or do you plan on showing me a little respect?"

He observed her reach inside and turn the water on. "My apologies. I didn't mean to give that impression."

"How else was I supposed to take it?" she interrogated.

He raised his hand over his shoulder, pointing his thumb behind him. "I'm going to hang out back here. It's not total privacy but I'll be out of the way enough that you'll not know I'm in the vicinity. If you need anything, then don't hesitate to speak up. I'd be glad to assist."

"I'm sure you would, but I like to think I do a decent job on my own. Thanks to a piece of shit sperm donor, I've got no reason to trust anything a man has to say," she remarked.

Casper cackled. "You're in luck. I'm not your sperm donor."

"Space. Please," she insisted, showing no humor toward his comment.

"Sure," he said, taking a few steps backwards. "Was just trying to lighten the mood."

She grabbed the towel, unfolded it once, and draped it over the top right side of the enclosure away from the water pelting down. She unfastened the skirt zipper fashioned at the hip and the loosened attire dropped to her feet without assistance. Sitting in the bottom of the staircase outside the room, Casper glanced over and couldn't take his eyes off her standing in just a silk blouse and blue lace panties. She grabbed the bottom sides of the blouse and pulled it up her body slowly. Clearing it from her head, she dropped the garment on the floor behind her. The first thing he recognized about her predominantly bare body was a tattoo on the bottom left side of her back. The pink seahorse was so low that its tail might possibly be inked on her buttock. He didn't know because the lower portion was hidden behind the panties. As much as he was enjoying the show, he looked the opposite direction when spotting her head turn slightly.

She glanced out the doorway over her shoulder and saw him staring toward the kitchen. She was thoroughly astonished that he wasn't goggling at her in panties. Initially, she felt relieved seeing him possess a respectable amount of self control, however, this appreciation wore off quickly after it occurred to her the reason he abstained from checking her out might be because he didn't see any attractive qualities. Suddenly infuriated, she snapped her head forward and bent over before ripping those panties to her ankles. Now she didn't care what he did but that small percentage of her yearning for attention wanted him to glimpse.

What she failed to realize was that when she stopped concentrating on him, Casper turned to the wall in front of him and barely noticed her commotion out of the corner of his eye. Strongly sensing her observance divert elsewhere, he peered through the doorway in time to catch the cute little panties hit the floor while her ass stuck out as she remained leaning forward. Then she stood up straight and removed one foot at a time from the center of the skirt and panties. He didn't know how old she was exactly but came to the conclusion that she was incredibly tone for her age.

He looked down in front of him and smiled when shaking his head. Sure, he had dealings with more women than he could keep count but something about Shei other than her ass stood out to him. He gathered she was feisty somehow, and it was a characteristic he liked. She radiated strength and independence. He was used to the lethargic personality type, so this was indisputably an exciting new experience.

Shei walked into the shower and closed the door. Hot water sprayed over her and its steaming heat caused her to step back. She looked around and saw the only personal hygiene product available was a bottle of men's body wash. Her stay was predetermined but no one bothered to supply her with feminine products.

"This is becoming a real shit show," she whispered under her breath. "I've got to walk around smelling like a fucking man. Gross."

Casper could not see her clearly through the stained glass. In fact, all that he could really make out was the blurred pink silhouette of her body meandering in one direction and then another as she presumably bathed.

Lacking shampoo to cleanse her hair properly, Shei slapped a thick gob of green goo on top of her head and rubbed through her hair until every fiber was covered with bubbly froth. She stepped forward into the fast downpour streaming overhead and drifted her hands through her hair again. The foam suds flowed down her face and shoulders after fading out of her hair. Shutting her eyes to prevent making Casper correct in the assumption that blinding herself would initiate his assistance, she washed the lathery residue off her face by leaning her head back and letting the water flow. Afterwards, she brought her head forward - opening her eyes and viewing the half tile wall. Her focus wasn't on that monotonous sight precisely. There was so much on her mind that the wall portrayed a blank canvas while she plunged into thoughts.

Things spiraled out of control so quickly that nothing made sense.

The vicious assault was the focal point and remained on her mind after happening. According to her father, everything was meant to transition effortlessly. Liam Rivera orchestrated a plan under his criminal persona and hired two goons with past convictions to abduct his daughter for ransom; however, Shei's role was to throw a twist in the plot and bring vengeance on her captor for a crime her father didn't feel received adequate punishment. Liam hired his own daughter to follow through on an offense she never dreamed herself capable of committing, and he assured her that all tracks would be untraceable. Her opinion was that all of this was a bad idea from the start. Unfortunately, she felt she must get involved when her motherly instincts kicked in after being informed her involvement pertained to serving justice for the murder of a ten year old child. If there was one thing with potential to push her over the edge, then reckless endangerment leading to the loss of a child's life may very well drive her to do the unthinkable.

She touched the damaged side of her face. Much of the pain abandoned her but the emotional trauma was still fresh. Her father would never allow a man to inflict physical abuse. Sierra's father never laid a hand on her but just his cursing and constant degradation invoked Liam to demand that Shei leave him. If he knew one of these men beat and bruised her, then she was certain the man responsible would pay dearly. Perhaps with his life.

As far as the man she was ordered to have a vendetta against, he was surprisingly treating her with decency. She envisioned disrespect, aggression, a foul mouth, and everything else associated with a hardened criminal. What she got was someone she could sense comfort and benevolence, which might make her assignment eminently difficult because he wasn't exhibiting signs of the deviant her father claimed him to be.

And those eyes!

Thinking about them sent her into a frenzy and caused her to lose focus on the task. Not to mention she found him handsome as well. Maybe she'd gone too long not having a man in her life and the current situation was all some delusional mistake. Despite what it was or wasn't, she stared at the wall but could only visualize his intense eyes gazing into the depths of her mind.

Casper heard the water stop and looked inside the bathroom. He noticed the towel missing from hanging over the enclosure. The glass door opened and she emerged, holding the towel wrapped around her. Wet hair bound together and stuck to her shoulders. All of her cosmetics were erased. She might not embrace her natural look with confidence but he admired the raw appearance. Truthfully, he saw pure natural beauty that didn't require assistance from lipstick and mascara. She kept her eyes on him while closing the door - possibly thinking he was anticipating she'd drop the towel at any second.

"I have you some clothes on the-"

"I saw them earlier. Thanks!" she interrupted.

"Yeah," he replied, giving her privacy by turning away. "I didn't find any panties for you to put on. The shirt and pants might not be your size but I grabbed what I thought would be comfortable. This place really doesn't have a lot to choose from."

Shei unfolded the towel from her back but kept her front areas covered. She continued to monitor him. Although she believed he was cute and a little charming, still she could not trust that he wasn't tempted to sneak a peek. Of course, there were moments when she wanted him to glimpse but she didn't want to make herself obvious. After patting her damp skin, she flipped the shirt aside and snatched the pants off the counter. Getting her legs inside them was a bit problematic since she was holding the towel against her at the same time, but she managed to get them on her waist and then went for the shirt. Putting the shirt on while keeping her breasts concealed required skill and her effort was effective. When sliding her head and one arm through their openings at once, the shirt lowered enough to cover the majority of one breast and she grabbed the towel with the opposite hand in order to squeeze the other arm through its sleeve. Now fully dressed, she glanced at Casper again and was baffled to see him continuing to look away. His lack of expressing curiosity really did begin to make her suspect she wasn't desirous.

Bending forward and scrubbing the towel against her head, she tried only with what she was capable of on her own to dry the hair since she didn't see a blow dryer anywhere. Several hard scrapes later, she dropped the towel and stood to glimpse at herself in the mirror. She recognized her hair wasn't necessarily presentable. It was tangly and all over the place.

"You knew a woman was coming here but didn't

provide the basic needs for her to take care of herself," she complained.

He stood out of the opening to the staircase and turned in time to see her approach through the doorway. On the one hand, those sweatpants were a little baggy but yet she filled them out nicely. On the other hand, the shirt came across as a couple of sizes too big but wasn't any different than how kids dressed nowadays. He honed in on her chest after detecting two tiny bulges inside the shirt. Clearly, her nipples were rock solid. In regard to the totality of her breasts, he saw they weren't much larger than if he put both his hands together to make a fist.

Afraid she'd catch him rubbernecking at her tits, he scanned around and behind her before targeting her eyes. "I searched this place high and low. Apparently, there's not been a lady here for some time because I didn't land across anything that might be useful to you."

She glowered at him straightaway. "Just great. This is going to be the most unpleasant stay of my life."

"Technically, it isn't supposed to be enjoyable," he specified.

She rolled her eyes and sighed. "Let's not get into the politics of things. All I'm saying is the least anyone could have done was acknowledge I'd be here."

He smirked schemingly. "Guess if that time of the month decides to hit, then you're going to have to plug it with toilet paper."

Her immediate backlash came in the form of her molding an uncongenial expression. "I'm beginning to think you're not as bad as people say. Don't fuck it up."

Ordinarily, he would have laughed at her response.

Instead, he preserved a straight face and reached inside his shirt breast pocket.

"Before it slips my mind," he said, pulling a gold chain attached to an Emerald stone from the pocket. "I'm meant to give you this."

Every speck of disapproval dropped from her face when shock took over abruptly. "That's my mother's necklace," she whispered softly.

He reached out, swaying the Emerald far below his fingers pinching the chain. "I was told you're supposed to wear it."

Her crestfallen eyes raised at him. "It's her birthstone. How did you get this?"

His lower lip bent out of shape before he bit the corner. "To be completely honest with you, we've got a lot of things to discuss and next moves to plan. With all of that being said, I think we should-"

"I don't care what you think!" she shrieked, shaking her head assertively. "Where did you get that?!"

He shrugged. "Your father ordered that I give it to you."

She shook her head again but with more aggression. "My father? Wait a minute. How do you have dealings with him, and why would he give you this to give to me? That's supposed to get handed down to my daughter."

"You're here for a reason and it's not what you think. You were told a bunch of shit just so you'd feel the need to get involved. I know what the deal is. In fact, I know why you think you're here," he confessed.

She swooped across and snatched the necklace dangling midair. Then she raised both hands in front of her with aggravation. "You haven't answered my question. How are you involved with my father? Nothing about any of this is making sense to me right now."

"I thought you didn't want to get into the politics of things?" he inquired.

"Dammit!" She held back tears but all the strained muscles in her face indicated she could fly off the handle at any moment. "Fill me in! Tell me what's going on."

He pressed his back on the wall next to the staircase. "Okay. I will tell you everything. Things you think you know, and a lot of stuff you don't. We're not going to talk about it right now though. We've got to concentrate on getting along with each other before we do anything."

"Tell me what your relations with my father involve and what you were doing with my mother's necklace," she growled.

Half his mouth sprung into a shit eating grin. "I see you're not one that likes to beat around the bush. But like I said earlier, once the steak is sizzling and we're-"

"My god! To hell with the steak," she viciously intervened.

He reared his head against the wall as if he was stunned by her outrage. He reached out slowly, presumptively attempting to touch the injured portion of her face.

Definitely not in the mood for sympathy, she slapped his arm back down beside him before he could get to her halfway. She gave a partial nod while squinting in her stare. The fact that he didn't react to her hostility spoke volumes in regard to how she was accustomed to seeing men respond. Of course, she was fortunate he wasn't like the few guys she had encountered. The top of her head was even with the bottom of his chest, and he was stocky that she could stand in front of him with an individual of her exact structure next to her just to span the width from one side of him to the other. If he was a raging wildman instead of this apparent giant teddy bear, then he would snap her in half without effort. Actually, he'd be competent to break every bone in the bodies of all the men that wronged her.

Fixated on his incredible eyes with their unnatural ability to mesmerize, she comprehended coherent sensibility in them. She found it so easy to recognize because the impression projected just in the way he looked at her. The majority of men would gawk at her inappropriately. Their eyes filled with thirst. Casper showcased nothing but a sense of genuine care. Something entirely new for her to encounter and process. She was starting to feel regretful about derogating his comments a moment ago. Perhaps he really was trying everything he knew how to comfort her and not override her with information likely to induce shock.

Too much confusion.

Uncertainty in everything.

Her only establishment was Casper not being the person she had been led to believe. At least he didn't resemble anything she was told. Now she was questioning if he was even the right man elected to participate in her abduction. What if the man who stuffed her in the trunk erroneously dropped her at the wrong location? An unfortunate mistake would breed catastrophic consequences. No! - she corrected herself. None of this could be a mistake because he spoke with Elliot when she was released to him. The two men talked like they knew what was going on.

Wrestling with the idea that she had no reason to fear, Shei unclipped the chain and raised it in front of him. Her lips drooped into a pitiful pout. "Sorry. I shouldn't take my frustration out on you. Think you might be able to hook this for me?"

He smiled wearily. "Sure. Anything you need. That's why I'm here."

She turned her back to him and arranged the damp, wavy lengths of hair in front of one shoulder. He reached in front of her, pulling the Emerald against her chest gently. His large fingers struggled opening the lock for a bit.

"Also, I think you're right. We shouldn't go down the rabbit hole just yet," she said.

His smile broadened but he didn't voice enjoyment. Alternatively, he continued to focus on trying to fasten that tiny clip.

Excited but also nervous to find out if his nature was to protect, Shei grinned too.

"I'm sure we've got plenty to talk about over those sizzling steaks," she concluded.

CHAPTER EIGHT

Beatrice Torres fetched her black Cardigan sweater draped on a peg of the coat rack mounted on the wall beside the front door. Short and round described her best. Cropped curly black hair. Brown eyes. A beast when it came to housekeeping in her golden years. After slipping into the wool sleeves, she reached for the green purse hanging on the same peg the Cardigan was suspended.

"You're positive you don't need me to stay and straighten up after dinner?" she asked, sliding the purse strap over her shoulder.

"Yes, dear. I've got no problem putting whatever leftovers away. The dishes can wait until tomorrow. I don't think you've got much left to do for the week anyway," Liam replied, standing across from her and holding a glass of dark liquor. He hadn't settled after the workday because he was still decked in office clothes.

"Tomorrow I plan to sanitize the half bath, if that's all right," she replied.

He swirled the alcohol inside the glass. "That will be fine. I don't use it often but with the little one staying, it could use a touch up. I'm sure she'll be in every room of the house. Which reminds me, I've got court tomorrow and am unsure what time I'll get out, so I'm going to need you to pick Sierra up after school."

"Ah, yes. I'll add that to my schedule," she mentioned, tapping one finger on the side of her head. "Sierra's never stayed overnight. Shei out of town or something?"

Liam reached up with the hand holding the glass and scraped the corner of his brow with one finger. "She's got herself in a unique situation. You know how girls are these days. Meet some dude hundreds of miles away online and then decide to meet, thinking he's everything that'll sweep her off her feet. She needed somewhere to drop the runt because she didn't want the distraction. Guess there wasn't anybody better than pawpaw."

Beatrice touched one hand against her chest. "Poor thing. That's terrible she wasn't included but I understand the reasoning. Do you know when Shei's supposed to get back?"

He lowered the drink after scratching his brow and gave it another swirl. "Hard to say when it comes to that girl. Everything she does is by the moment. She could be gone for three days or four weeks. Depends. I worry about her all the time; she's going to get mixed up with some douchebag because that seems to be the only type she attracts."

"If you need help with the little one for whatever reason, then I'd have no problem-"

"Betty! Betty! Betty!" Sierra squalled excitedly, running into the foyer from another room with her arms out in front of her while barreling toward her grandfather's precious handmaiden.

Beatrice's eyes widened and she extended her arms also, anticipating embracing the child. "Hey, sweetheart.

Come and give Aunt B some loving before I leave for the day."

She was of no relation to the Rivera family but *Aunt B* was a fitting nickname since she was engaged with them frequently. Every day except weekends, really. The moniker was self-proclaimed and no one - not even Sierra - called her by it.

The child bumped against Beatrice without attempting to stop and nearly knocked her off balance and against the door. She wrapped her little arms around her as far as they'd reach and squeezed.

"Are you coming back?" Sierra asked.

Beatrice patted her back. "I'll be here tomorrow, honey."

Liam sipped from his glass while observing their interaction. "That's enough, Sierra. Go wash your hands and get ready for dinner," he ordered.

"I don't want her to go!" Sierra shrieked.

"Aww," Beatrice sounded off, pressing the child against her.

"Sierra, pawpaw told you to do something. I don't want to send you to bed without eating," he said.

"Mister Rivera, be easy on her. She's only a child," Beatrice pleaded.

"Please, Beatrice. Don't make this any more difficult. She needs to learn to obey rules under my supervision," he stated.

She nodded and scowled at the same time. "Yes, sir. Guess I'd better get going. Have dinner of my own to prepare."

"No!" Sierra squalled.

"Sierra, get ready for dinner," he demanded.

A loud bang struck the door behind Beatrice. She glanced back over her shoulder and then turned to Liam. Whatever befuddlement in her mind percolated on her face.

"Are you expecting someone?" she inquired.

He leaned his head back proudly. "I have an associate arriving to discuss important business over dinner. Sierra will be fine. My meeting will only take a quick minute. Enough time to enjoy the decent meal you have prepared, chat a little about affairs, and then I'll see him on his way. I have the evening well under control."

"If you say so," she replied, prying Sierra's tiny arms off her and pushing the child away. "I've just never known you to bring the job home."

"We had a last minute encounter and didn't get to discuss the circumstance, so I asked him to come over this evening to go over details. It's an urgent matter we've got to debate before tomorrow. Can't be stumbling into the courthouse and not know which direction things are going," he mentioned.

"I understand. Caught me off guard is all," she said.

A second intense knock slammed the door.

Beatrice winced. "You two must get along pretty well. He's about as impatient as you are."

She turned, opened the door, and was engrossed in shock. The man standing in front of her was not what she expected to greet. She thought he'd be a handsome, clean-shaven attorney. What she found was a man who didn't quite meet her expectations. He was smooth-faced like she imagined, however, something about his natural attributes in the flesh emanated devilry. His tautened eyes and rugged grin intensified her impression of him. He wasn't attractive either. His khakis were wrinkled as if he slept in them for days and the button-up shirt reminded her of the cheap type put on straight out of the plastic packaging because of it having creases in particular places.

Still unable to speak due to her sudden surprise, she just looked at him and hoped her face didn't show consternation the way she felt it.

"Howdy, ma'am," Elliot said kindly.

"Can I help you?" she asked point-blank, uncertain this individual was the same man that Liam was scheduled to meet. She was outright skeptical because he didn't resemble the type of person Liam would associate himself with. The guy mirrored the kind that Liam spent long days making sure were put away.

"You sure can," he answered, smiling wildly. "I'm looking for Rivera. Liam Rivera."

"Oh. Okay," she said quietly, trying not to gush disheartedness. "You're at the right place."

"Hmm. If I'm at the correct address, then what am I still doing standing out here?" he queried.

Beatrice didn't know how to respond. There was no doubt his words were impudent but he delivered them in a modest tone.

"Come inside! You don't have to stand out there and wait for my approval!" Liam's cogent voice blasted past her with authority she could not condemn.

"We both know you ain't gotta tell me twice!" Elliot responded back. His wretched voice also drilled beyond her.

He slid sideways through the slim gap between

Beatrice and the trim of the doorway since she didn't step aside to approve his entrance. He laid his hand on top of her shoulder and leaned toward the side of her head in passing. "You ain't gotta be so timid with me. I'm just a working-class man following the guidance of Mister Rivera here."

Beatrice didn't speak. She didn't step out of the way and give him more space to cross. Perhaps she was frozen and mute because perturbation forbade her to engage in dissension.

"I was seriously starting to wonder about you when I didn't get anything back from my text," Liam confessed.

Elliot cleared Beatrice before stopping to look around for a moment and admire the scenery. "I don't answer texts. They leave a trace. If any heat was to catch up with me, then all authorities would have to do is provide a warrant to my service provider for a copy of call logs and messages. I prefer doing things face to face."

Liam raised his glass to that remark. "You are an intelligent man in the way you think. I see why I made you my number one."

Finally, Beatrice turned toward the men after her sudden shock subdued. "Are you positive that you don't need me to stay and look after Sierra? You'd be able to talk business and not have to worry about keeping an eye on her."

"No, Beatrice. I don't need you to stay and rack up the overtime. We have very sensitive matters to speak about and it's best if you went home," Liam stated.

Elliot looked back at her and smiled crookedly, offering a better view of his uneven tar stained teeth. "I'll keep a good close eye on her.”

Still partly uncomfortable with his arrival, she felt his comment further distress the mind. Beatrice couldn’t bring herself to look at him again. The vibe was intense and she could not shake it off. With no intent to associate herself, she turned and proceeded to go on her way.

“I’ll see you bright and early in the morning, dear!” Liam mentioned.

Quietly, she stepped outside and closed the door behind her.

“She wasn’t supposed to see you. The last thing we need is a slip up,” Liam uttered.

“I take her as a sweet, considerate little old lady. She isn’t worried about me, and will probably forget my face by tomorrow,” Elliot defended.

“Speaking of slip ups and not being seen; you were witnessed dragging my daughter across the back lawn. It was reported to the damn police. I told you to make sure you stayed invisible,” Liam whispered, keeping his voice low to prevent the risk of having Sierra hear him in the next room.

Elliot chuckled forcibly. “How was I gonna avoid that happening? We were out in the middle of broad daylight. Naturally, someone was gonna see something. Why hasn’t the shit made it onto the radio or news? I haven’t heard anybody talk about it.”

Liam sighed. “Things are silent at my request. I’m highly respected, you know? The media believes if they broadcast what’s going on, then whoever has her might demand ransom. Or decide to take her out of state altogether. The police are working quietly. Unfortunately, she'll be reported as missing to the public after seventy-two hours and that's when the massive manhunt begins. But we're a step ahead of every procedure they put in place. Just be sure to make it where no trace of her will ever be found."

"What about dude?" Elliot inquired.

"Casper?" Liam asked.

"Yeah. Whoever that is with her," Elliot said.

"I don't care what you do. You can string him out in the wilderness and give wild animals something to gnaw on," Liam replied, smirking. "By the way, is he still under the assumption it's up to him to close the deal?"

Elliot nodded. "Yes, sir. I even told him to be sure he gets the job done. What about your ole girl; she still got the impression she's the Saving Grace in the matter?"

"She is. Which is best because she'll not see what's coming. Neither will Casper. I never cared much for him anyway," Liam stated.

"I think he got the hots for her pretty quick. Didn't waste no time jumping in there to defend her," Elliot disclosed.

"What do you mean?" Liam whispered. His voice turned strict all of a sudden.

"I may have had some fun with her, okay. I certainly did when I picked her up. Had to make her a tad bit scared. Let her know she's playing with the big boys," Elliot confessed.

"I swear, if you-"

"Pawpaw!" Sierra yelled from another room.

Liam strained his eyes at him. "Keep in mind that we will have this conversation at another time, because I do not appreciate everything I just heard. Right now is dinner time though. When the child is ready, then we must go. Wouldn't be advisable to cause her to wait."

Elliot extended one arm toward the doorway behind Liam. "Then by all means, let's not keep the little princess waiting."

"My granddaughter will be joining us, so we'll have to speak in code. This shouldn't be too much of a problem though; she'll not have any idea what we're talking about," Liam addressed, turning his back to him.

The men navigated into a spacious dining area where the table - made to seat eight individuals - stood before a large window covered with a thin purple curtain. More food than they could eat adorned the table. There was barbeque chicken strips, ham, mashed potatoes, green beans, fried squash, deviled eggs, and sliced pineapple. These were just things Elliot noticed at first glance, so there might be more he hadn't recognized. This grand celebration of Liam bidding farewell to his own flesh and blood pleased Elliot's sadistic sense of humor that he smiled.

Sitting across the table and next to the chair on the end was Sierra. She was decked in pajamas and her hair in a ponytail. Beside her bare plate lay a little brown rabbit stuffed animal and on the opposite side was a glass filled with some type of blue juice.

Elliot had never seen the child before now. He analyzed her closely, noticing she favored her mother's features a lot. The facial similarities sent his mind echoing the visualization of slamming Shei's bagged head onto the floor. Since he didn't have children or hang around anyone that did, he didn't know of a polite way to approach Sierra and so he didn't say anything. Instead, he stood behind the chair across from her and silently praised the feast laid out ahead of him.

"Get your bath, sweetheart?" Liam asked softly, approaching a small two door wooden cellarette on the side of the room away from the table.

"Yeah. Betty made me take one when she was cooking," Sierra chirped.

"Good deal. It's bedtime after dinner because pawpaw is going to have a very busy day tomorrow," he stated, opening the doors and revealing various brands of clear and dark liquor. "Elliot, do you care for a drink?"

Elliot glanced back and could only see Liam's hindside blocking the cellarette. "Sure! That's not an offer I'd be willing to turn down."

Liam reached for one of the clear liquor bottles. "How does White Rum sound?"

"Sounds like a winner," Elliot replied.

After retrieving two glasses from the holder mounted inside the door, and filling them almost to the brim, Liam walked to the table and sat one glass down in front of the chair on the end between Sierra and Elliot. He reached the other glass out for his associate to take.

"It isn't the best I could provide but it will give a kick," he said.

Elliot wasted no time accepting the offer. "Thanks. It's better than not receiving anything."

"Sweetheart, I'd like to introduce you to our new friend Elliot," Liam said, pulling out the chair in front of him.

"Hi," she greeted, waving at their new friend at the

same time.

"Hey," Elliot replied quietly, lacking liveliness in his tone.

Liam took a seat and scooted himself toward the table. He picked up the napkin laying across his plate, unfolded it, and tucked it inside the front of his shirt collar before reaching down and flattening the lower portion on his chest.

He looked at Elliot, who was the last person standing. "You can have a seat. Make yourself at home."

Elliot took a drink from the glass before sitting it down and pulling the chair out.

Finally, everyone was seated. Liam scoured the table, studying each dish individually since he didn't know what all Beatrice prepared for the evening. He wasn't surprised by the amount of food because she did this every few days. She'd cook enough to have leftovers in order to spend other days taking on duties throughout the house. There never was much to do but she repeated the routine regardless.

"What would you like first, sweetheart?" he asked.

"Mac and cheese!" Sierra exclaimed.

"I'm sorry, honey, but that isn't one of the choices. Beatrice didn't make any this time. I should have told her you were coming and she would've made your favorite. I'll remind her next time," he said.

She stood on her knees in the chair and scanned the table.

"Do you want some ham?" he asked.

She nodded overdramatically.

He picked up two slices and slapped them on her

plate. Afterwards, he licked the syrupy honey glaze off his fingers and glimpsed at Elliot.

"Dig in. You don't need my permission," he encouraged. "There is more than enough to go around."

"I'm not used to hospitality," Elliot mentioned.

Liam looked at Sierra again. "Want some chicken strips?"

She smiled. "Yes!"

He scooped a few pieces with a large serving spoon and moved them onto her plate. Then he returned to the aluminum tray and picked up a few more strips before going back to her plate and dumping them.

"What else do you want, darling?" he asked, laying the spoon in the tray.

"Nothing," she chirped, sliding her knees out from under her and sitting properly.

"Nothing? You've got to eat more than just ham and chicken, honey. You're a growing girl," he mentioned.

"Nah," she replied quickly.

Elliot stretched forward and grabbed the spoon in the tray of chicken strips. "She doesn't wanna eat, then I ain't got no problem taking her share."

Liam shot a nasty glance at him. "She's just a child."

"As was I once," Elliot mumbled, obviously not denying children the experience of his smartass personality.

Both men began piling their plates with as much food as they could hold. Unsurprisingly, Elliot wasn't satisfied with accumulating just one layer. He stacked ham upon mashed potatoes and deviled eggs on top of fried squash. Sierra nibbled on a strip of barbeque chicken while watching the men continue to supply their rapacious hunger.

Liam winked at Elliot with the eye furthest from Sierra. "When you go hunting tomorrow, it might be best to do it a little before dark. Not too late though; you're going to want to be able to see what you're after. I imagine you're not much for checking in game, so holding off until late evening will stop anyone from seeing your prey and will also give mother nature time to clear your tracks before next sunrise."

Elliot took a fierce bite from a slice of ham. "I like how you think, boss. We really are a lot alike. That's exactly how I was thinking about doing it. But what if for some reason I land off target?"

Liam sneered. "Hmm. Collateral damage in a sense. I don't suppose it would be too big of a deal as long as it was easily repairable."

Elliot crammed the rest of the ham slice inside his mouth. "I don't plan on missing but I had to ask," he said, chewing.

"And you do know none of this ever gets talked about?" Liam inquired.

"I've never kissed and told any affairs I've been involved with in my life. What I do stays between you and me. My only concern is you guaranteeing me that I'll be in the clear of everything when this is over," Elliot stated, seizing his glass of alcohol.

"Don't worry about anything. I'll get the paperwork taken care of and have your scheduled appearance taken out of the system tomorrow," Liam confirmed.

Sudden coughing disrupted the conversation. Liam

looked at Sierra and immediately recognized her choking because she was leaning over her plate, mouth open and face turned red. She continued to cough, trying to dislodge whatever was caught in her throat. Liam raised from his seat but not entirely and reached behind her before smacking her hard on the back, several times. Then he picked up the glass of blue juice with the other hand and raised it to her mouth.

"Drink some Kool-Aid, honey. It'll make it go down," he suggested.

She might not have wanted to do what he requested but didn't have a choice when he tilted the glass against her lips.

Sierra swallowed.

"It's gone!" she groaned hoarsely.

He removed the glass from her mouth and placed it on the table. "You've got to be more careful. Can't be going and scaring me like that."

"When I was a kid, I was told not to drink the Kool-Aid," Elliot commented dryly.

She looked at him with watery eyes.

"Don't tell her things like that," Liam snapped, taking a seat again. "What is wrong with you?"

"It was a joke, ha-ha. That whole Jonestown deal," Elliot said.

"I know what you were referring to and it wasn't-"

"I want mommy," Sierra sobbed.

"Look what you've done," Liam hissed, smacking the table. He stopped everything for a moment to gather himself and then focused on his frightened granddaughter.

"Sweetheart, mommy isn't here. She left you with

me and took off. Pawpaw isn't going to let anything happen to you."

"When is she coming back?" Sierra whined.

"I don't know. She took off with someone. I'll let you speak to her if she calls. If she doesn't, then we'll focus on making the most of our time together. You want to make some good memories with pawpaw, don't you?" he asked.

She wiped the tears from her eyes and shook her head. "Yeah," she answered quietly.

Elliot ingested a large amount of Rum and rattled off a noisy breath as the slow burn progressed down into his gut. Then he hiccuped. "What made you wanna pair up? I'm intrigued. What do you get out of this?"

Liam held a spoonful of mashed potatoes in front of him but Elliot's inquiry didn't give him the chance to enjoy it. "Would you like for me to show you?"

Elliot simpered. "I sure would."

Liam laid the spoon on his plate without taking the bite before ripping away the napkin tucked in his shirt and dropping it on the table. He pushed his chair back and stood, stepping aside and advancing behind Elliot to embark in the direction of the doorway to the next room.

"Let me grab it. I'll be right back," he said, patting Elliot's shoulder.

One on one with the child, Elliot didn't know what to say to eliminate creating an awkward situation.

Sierra picked up a ham slice and scrubbed her tongue along one side, licking off a large section of honey glaze. "My pawpaw gets rid of bad people. Are you a superhero too?"

He laughed momentarily. "A superhero?"

Her eyes broadened while staring at him from behind the piece of ham blocking the lower portion of her face. "Yeah. Like Superman and Batman, and Catwoman. My pawpaw works with them. They make all the bad people go away."

"Ya know, I also make people go away," he responded, thinking quickly.

Her curiosity flared when she asked, "Bad people?"

He smiled. "I guess you could say that. Everyone does something bad though. Some people just do worse things than others. I make people do things they're supposed to do. If they don't, then they disappear."

"So you are one," she whispered in wonderment.

"This here should tell you everything you need to know," Liam said, emerging from the doorway,

Elliot looked at him and saw that he was carrying a white business size envelope. Catching a few brief glimpses as the envelope faced various directions during Liam's approach, he didn't recognize any lettering on the front that spelled out either a sender or recipient address.

"What is that?" he asked, keeping his eyes on it.

"You'll see it's everything within my reasoning," Liam answered, dodging details due to the child in the room.

"Pawpaw, he fights bad people too!" Sierra squealed.

Liam paused following her remark - hesitant to take another step toward the table. "What did you tell her?"

Elliot sighed, possibly frustrated with Liam apparently lacking trust. "Nothing, man. She asked if I was a superhero, so I told her that I make people go away if

80

they don't cooperate."

"Ah," he sounded out, and approached the table once more. He looked at Sierra and grinned. "He's one of the best there are. Has put away more bad guys than anyone I know."

She giggled excitedly. "Really?!"

Elliot watched the envelope slide over his shoulder and grabbed it as it was let go when Liam crossed behind the chair. Bringing it down in front of him, he raised the unsealed flap and removed a couple of loose pages folded together. He opened their double folds and the first thing he spotted on the top of the first page was that this document was actually beneficiary information pertaining to a life insurance policy. Beneath the company name and logo was two blocks, one underneath the other and both taking up the top and bottom of the page. The blocks contained pertinent information such as name, address, birthdate, social security number, and other relevant forms of personal identification. He noticed the name in the top section was that of a Priscella Robyn Rivera.

"Your wife?" he asked.

"Yes, sir," Liam replied, taking his seat and reaching for the napkin first thing.

Elliot scanned diagonally to the right side of the page and was automatically bowled over by seeing the policyholder amount of two million dollars. He wanted to say something but all of those zeros glued to his eyes made him speechless. It was the first time in his life he'd got this close to two million bucks. Honestly, he'd never seen as much as ten thousand at once. He glimpsed at the lower block, despite how difficult it was to take his eyes off that dollar amount, and saw the recipient's name spelled out clearly. The beneficiary was none other than Sierra Rayne Allen. He assumed the last name differential was the result of Shei signing Sierra's father's last name on the birth certificate.

Eying across all of Sierra's personal information, he reached the one bracket that was a particular interest to him. The section stated how much she would receive in the event of her grandmother's passing, and it was the full two million. He flipped to the next sheet but found no further information provided on the blank page.

He nodded and brought the pages together, folding them the way they were received. "Yeah. Looks like you're sitting on a gold mine."

"That's a fact," Liam affirmed, reengaging with the spoonful of mashed potatoes. "But the way it's set up is there's eleven more years before it can be accessed."

"I'm following," Elliot stated, sliding the document back inside the envelope. "But why isn't the parental party listed?"

"That guardian wanted it set up this way so the beneficiary would have a comfortable start to life when coming of age. It would also pay for whatever college education the recipient chose to pursue," Liam replied.

Elliot laid the envelope on the table and slid it toward him slowly. "What's your plan with all this?"

Liam smiled like he was thrilled to mention the genius details. "Seeing that I'll need full custody to make the proper adjustments, that's the first step. The rest is smooth sailing. I'll file an official document with the court, seeking to amend the policy to begin sending monthly payments immediately, and have Judge Reyes sign the order. I will take full control of the funds and the intended recipient will never learn of the matter. Not even after eleven years from now."

"What's a *recepant*?" Sierra asked.

Liam flashed his best illusional expression of delight when chuckling at her inability to say the word correctly. "It's recipient, sweetheart, and it basically means collector."

Elliot showed no softness toward the child's humorous curiosity. "Why didn't the policyholder list the spouse? That would've made more sense and none of this would be happening," he inquired stone heartedly.

"My- Umm. It was decided before signing the policy that the spouse, being the head of household and provider for the insured, shouldn't be rewarded in the death of their significant other. The agreement was that any such payout would get divided amongst grandchildren. Seeing how it turned out being just one, there's nothing to split which makes my vision all the more realistic. The last ingredient is what you've been employed to do," Liam said.

Elliot raised what was now a half glass of liquor. "Yeah. About that, the cost of my involvement just went up."

"What do you mean went up?" Liam asked distastefully.

"Ole dude isn't gonna see the share he thinks he's getting because he's out of the deal. I want his part. No, I'm taking his part. Thirty thousand is less than reasonable for what you want me to do," Elliot answered.

"I'm taking your charges away," Liam retaliated snappily. "What more do you expect from me?"

Elliot took a sip from the glass while eyeing the child across from him. He broke away from drinking and lowered it on the table. "You could wait eleven years to watch her flourish, or you can give me what I want and it all be yours. Gonna be impossible to pull this off without me."

Liam sighed heavily with aggravation. "All right. Fine. Thirty grand but not a penny more, and do not ask me for anything else."

Elliot pulled a deviled egg to his mouth, smiled, and raised his brows. "You're not gonna know I exist after this is done. I'm gonna head out west somewhere and pick up a new life."

Sierra giggled, watching him cram the whole half egg inside his mouth and cause one cheek to bulge while holding it tucked away.

"That's funny," she mentioned.

He looked at her without expression and withdrew the egg from pressing against his jaw. Then he began to chew, while possibly dissatisfied with the notion that he unintentionally entertained her.

CHAPTER NINE

Casper jabbed a fork into the slab of meat cooking in the skillet and flipped it raw side down. Grease crackled and popped around the chunk of cattle flesh. In a separate pan on the burner beside the one frying steak was a combination of sliced onions and green bell peppers. The vegetables were still raw since the burner was not turned on. Perhaps he was waiting closer to the time for the steaks to be done since sauteing would take only about fifteen minutes, if he did everything correctly. He skipped heating the skillet for five minutes prior to adding the vegetables and olive oil, so he wasn't really sure what to expect.

Shei sat on the far side of the island, facing the kitchen. The strong aroma of steak frying extended beyond the kitchen and caused her to crave dinner with an increasing hunger. Her evening with Casper had gone so well in the natural sense that she nearly forgot that all of this was linked to her abduction. He didn't treat her the way a captor should. Instead, he was very polite and spoke to her like he genuinely cared not about the situation but the condition of her well-being.

Since his back was to her, she didn't mind broadening her observation of him by checking his ass in those snug fitting jeans. She didn't think sexually but did give him a nine out of ten ranking for having a cute ass.

With regard to sexuality, she had gone so long without passion that it didn't cross her mind. Plenty of opportunities to have dirty ideas flood her head but the only one that struck her was that he'd probably look pretty appetizing in a Calvin Klein commercial, advertising a pair of boxer briefs. Just that unusual thought spawned her to smile.

He opened the dishwasher under the opposite side of the sink and pulled out the top rack. "Want something to drink?" he asked, removing two long stem wine glasses and sitting them on the counter.

"Sure. What are you offering?" she inquired.

He turned and pointed a finger at her while on his way to the refrigerator. "That I've got no idea yet."

"Are you sure this isn't your place?" she asked.

"I'm positive," he replied, opening the door on the refrigerator. "There is no way I could afford a place like this. I'm employed with a temp agency, making fourteen an hour. I can barely afford an apartment. Whoever owns this property, they're in a much better position than me."

He looked from one shelf to the next, rummaging his sight through a ridiculous amount of food and condiments. Whoever owned this place obviously didn't mind abandoning the expensive display of perishable items. There were beef patties, bratwurst, Bluefin tuna, and Sirloin. All of which would expire in a matter of days since they hadn't been stored in the freezer. Even the unopened gallon of milk might be in its final days.

He hunched over slightly and peered upon the third shelf. Finally, he found what he was looking for. There were three wine bottles laying toward the back with their necks facing him. He reached inside and grabbed a bottle at random since he wasn't able to read the labels and distinguish if they were different flavors. He glanced at it for a second and then turned to let her see.

"Does Pahlmeyer work for you?" he asked.

Just one name on the bottle was large and clear enough for her to notice from where she was sitting. "Jayson?" she asked.

He looked at it again. "Yeah. That's what it says."

"Red wine?" she further inquired.

He scrunched his face. "Should I pick a different one? I'm okay with anything but I don't want to pour something you're not crazy about."

"No. That one is fine. I was just thinking how expensive it is. Those bottles are like sixty dollars a pop," she stated.

Casper laughed and swung the refrigerator door shut. "Then I don't guess this is going to be the typical dinner. Expensive wine. One of the best steak varieties money can buy. We've got our own private restaurant operating here."

She giggled but it wasn't nearly as infinite as her smile. "Not even close to personal. If this is how far someone would go to get a date with me, then I will be happy to stay single."

"This definitely isn't my idea of a date," he voiced, pulling open one of the drawers beneath the counter beside the sink and taking out a corkscrew bottle opener.

"Oh, really? Now I'm interested. What does an ideal date mean to you?" she asked curiously.

He peeled back the paper concealing the cork. "The night would begin by stopping for a few bacon cheeseburgers, two large fries, and a couple of fountain drinks. Then I'd take us to some peaceful nighttime overlook where we'd talk, listen to music, and enjoy our greasy food. This whole wining and dining thing wouldn't cross my mind."

She laughed at his response. "The cheap guy really does exist."

"Come on now," he said jokingly, throwing his head back after twisting the corkscrew down inside the pulp. "There's nothing wrong with my idea. Tell me one problem you see with it."

Still grinning, Shei rolled her eyes. "You honestly think a girl wants fast food and to sit in the dark somewhere, listening to whatever music you like? If the two of you didn't speak enough leading up to the date, then don't you think that not speaking to each other while just sitting there would turn stale - like really quick?"

He pried the cork from the bottle and poured the first glass. "I wouldn't think so. I don't see anything wrong with just chilling and listening to the radio. Some girls might find that romantic. You never know."

"A dollar burger isn't going to get anyone a second date. I don't care how attractive I find the guy. Just saying," she admitted.

Casper set the bottle on the counter after filling the second glass and picked up the first one. Holding that one glass, he snatched the fork and turned the steak in the skillet again. Afterward, he dispatched the silverware onto the section of stovetop between both pans and turned the left side oven dial slightly to start heating the sliced vegetables.

He turned and gave her an oblique smart aleck smile. "I'd love to know where you can get a burger for a dollar these days."

Her face quickly displayed a baffled expression. "Out of everything I said, that's all you took from it?"

"No. That isn't the only thing," he refuted, placing the glass on the island counter and sliding it across to her. "I've learned you're not into simple things. Stuff needs to be done a particular way or else you're not interested."

She frowned. "That's not how I meant for it to come out."

He raised both hands with palms forward and shrugged. "It's okay. This is too screwed up of a situation for us to be discussing what our dating preferences are anyway. We come from two polar opposite backgrounds. You enjoy the way things are done for you, and I'm happy with how I do things."

"Weirdly, we're starting to sound like two people in a relationship," she declared.

He tensed his lips to one side and turned his back on her slowly. "Wow. Don't start talking like that. I'm not in the position to ever see myself with anybody. My past has more flaws than I can overcome."

She seemed to knock back his self-doubt when switching the subject rather abruptly by asking, "You're holding me hostage, so why don't you have me tied up or locked in a room? Aren't you afraid I'll try to get away?"

He grabbed the silicone spatula off the counter and commenced pushing it through the vegetables before tossing and turning them from one area to another constantly. "I'm not worried about you going anywhere.

There's no place to go. We've got nothing but woods all around us. Mountains."

"True, but the road I came in on does lead back to someplace," she said.

Casper snickered. "Maybe so; however, the important issue in all this is you and I both know you're not going anywhere. What you don't know is that I'm aware you volunteered yourself to be kidnapped. Sorry, wrong choice of word. You accepted being hired for this. Assault and battery was not part of the agreement though. Now I'm as mindfucked as you are about what's really going on. The deeper it goes, the more senseless it gets."

She tilted her head just a bit to one side and two shallow crinkles structured between her eyes when her face suddenly became distorted. "Hold on. What gives you the ridiculous notion that I'd deliberately subject myself to this nonsense?"

"Because we're working for the same person," he explained, plunging the fork in the steak before moving it from the skillet and over onto a plate behind his glass and the wine bottle. There was a second plate with a thick slab of fried meat on it already, so it seemed the only thing left was to finish sauteing the vegetables.

"Doesn't make sense that your father has us both involved, but what's most unsettling about this whole mess is that I was hired to make you disappear and your job is to kill me. If you compare what we were told to do, then it appears to be a plan designed for neither of us to make it out," he added.

Shei's mouth dropped open. This unforeseen revelation totally blindsided her. She didn't know if she was more embarrassed than shocked, or vice versa. "Holy shit! How do you know what I'm supposed to do?"

Keeping his back to her, Casper continued to stir those darkened onions and peppers. "Your father told me everything you're supposed to do. A two night and three day stay, pretending to play this role of victim in distress; which, by the way, you completely suck at portraying. On the second night - tomorrow night if you want to get technical about it - you are supposed to murder me. I don't know how but that's the gist of the plan you were told. Get rid of me over some vendetta your father has against my past. You don't know the full truth though. His plan was to pay you and pull off one massive cover-up that would jeopardize his reputation and all parties involved if the truth got out."

The more he admitted being aware of her purpose, the more uncomfortable and doublecrossed she felt. She didn't have any bad feelings toward Casper because he hadn't done anything to make their time together awkward or aggravating. If anything, his generosity caused her to question why she agreed to follow through with the plan in the first place.

All of her ill will was toward her father. He gave her specific orders. She did not support this vile plot initially, but Liam assured her that survival by means of self-defense would yield no consequences. The truth was a grim secret never to be known. Casper's shocking admittance changed everything. Shei felt violated - stripped of appreciation she thought her father felt for her while outright oblivious to whatever new and true agenda. As if she were the recipient of amnesia following the blast from a landmine, she was defeated, deceived, and uniformed of the truth.

"Well this utterly guts my purpose for being here. Why would he tell you these things when you're the target?" she asked.

"Because the plan I was given that involves you is similar," he retorted, scraping half the vegetables onto one plate before moving to the next and emptying the skillet.

She thought about one of his prior comments, constructing an understanding as it all came back to her gradually. "Wait just a second. You said your job is to make me disappear. What do you mean? I thought you were supposed to be under the impression you're holding me for ransom."

"No. Your father wanted you under the impression that that's what I assumed. He had to tell you something convincing or you wouldn't have put yourself in this spot. I don't particularly like being the one to break the news but he assigned me the same deal," he said.

"Which is?" she asked dreadfully.

He turned with a plate in each hand and approached the island. Sitting one on the side nearest him, he reached over and carefully placed the other in front of her. Then he backtracked and nabbed his glass and the wine bottle off the counter.

"There's no point in me saying any more. I think you get the meaning," he said.

"Tell me," she blurted spunkily.

He sat the bottle off to the side between them but kept a grip on the glass while taking his seat. "Okay. The truth is, your father lured you here to have you killed. He spent a couple of months planning how to do it without having direct involvement himself. Being a prosecuting attorney, he had all the resources to enlist the right people. At least he thought. I'm not here to fulfill his wish, and I have no desire to harm you. I've got my own situation to sort out."

"Bullshit." She scorched him with disbelief.

"For what purpose would he request that you wear your mother's necklace?" he asked.

His question prompted her to reach up and grasp the gemstone hanging against her chest. "My father would never endanger me. He flips out and threatens to annihilate a guy just for talking to me the wrong way."

Casper took a drink before sitting the glass next to his plate. "Do you think he may have played the part to gain your trust?"

She puckered her face in contempt. "Hell no. I've been his little princess all my life. The one guy I was in a committed relationship with, my father literally wanted to kill him."

Casper sighed. Perhaps he dreaded knowing what he said next could go either way. "I don't want you to panic and take your aggravation out on me, but we need to discuss your mother's life insurance policy. What it means to you. How it's set up. Anything you can think of."

Tears filled her eyes when the conversation shifted to her mother. "Can we not talk about her? I was very close to my mother and it just hurts thinking about everything."

"Dammit, I need you to think," he remarked insensitively.

Still holding the gemstone since it was the closest she could get to her mom, she reached up and swept away a few tears that escaped her will to hold back. "I've got nothing to do with her policy. It's set up to go to my daughter after she turns eighteen. What does that have to do with anything?"

"You're not a natural when it comes to seeing things transparently, are you?" he inquired.

"I think I'm decent at seeing through bullshit; however, I don't quite follow what you're hinting at with this conversation," she answered.

He bowed his head, concentrating on sifting his fork through the vegetables. "I don't know how to sugarcoat what needs to be said, so I'm just going to say it like it is. Your father doesn't want the funds going to your daughter when she turns eighteen. He devised this plan to take on the responsibility of being her primary caretaker and become the successor of the trust. He's got a lot of people on his side to make this happen. He'll completely bleed those funds that she'll never know were hers. In fact, she'll likely never even learn about it."

"That's absurd. My father might be a lot of things but he isn't savage. I feel ridiculous for almost allowing myself to entertain the idea," she vented.

He stopped stirring the vegetables and laid his fork down. "This is not something I would lie to you about. Liam Rivera offered to clear my record and provide a bonus of fifteen thousand dollars, if I took you out of the equation."

"Right. You honestly expect me to buy that?" she asked sarcastically.

Then she nudged the plate of untouched food to the center of the island and stood from her stool. Pure skepticism contorted her face worse than any prior suspicion.

"Coming from a guy that fought to lie his way through a trial involving the murder of a child, I don't believe anything," she commented.

He pulled his fist to his chin and then slammed it down beside his plate. "I didn't kill anyone. I've got proof of that."

"Sure you do. That's why you spent - *how many years?* - locked up over the evidence against you," she replied, passing him after crossing the side of the island.

"Hey, aren't you going to eat?" he questioned.

"Nah. I'm not hungry anymore," she communicated, approaching the short passage between the kitchen and bathroom.

Shei didn't know where to go.

She didn't know the layout of the property.

The only thing she knew to do was turn left and chance whatever discovery at the top of the stairs. It was the furthest she could go to be alone after all. She didn't want to be in any place where Casper was visible. Obviously, her sense of comfort toward him had diminished.

Casper brought his hands together and tucked them beneath his chin. The thought of pursuing her failed to cross his mind. Honestly, he was as sidetracked by her sudden outburst as she was resentful of his revelation. These next few days were going to be more complicated than he originally perceived. Gaining her trust by providing the wretched truth was his key to defeating Liam's fraud against him; unfortunately, he seemed to have a long way to go to master the lock.

There had to be something ultimately convincing enough to alter her perception that didn't involve him widening the distance between them with his inconceivable honesty.

Liam Rivera might be one of the state's top prosecuting attorney's, but it was impossible that he didn't mistakenly leave a trace of prejudicial evidence.

This was a matter of proving the devil's guilt.

Outside of the playground disguised as a dictatorial legal system.

CHAPTER TEN

She lay on her stomach on the bed in the room she claimed without asking. Looking out the large half moon shaped window behind the iron rod headboard, she angrily admired the picturesque backdrop of the sun all but extinguished behind the mountain tops miles away. If this had been a meaningful romantic getaway, then such natural resources would have served as an essential aphrodisiac for bonding moods. However, she was in no position to experience harmony, and aggravation was grandiose.

There was too much on her mind and none of it supported a positive outlook.

Her mother's unbearable battle with cancer which ultimately ended in death.

The violent morning ambush.

Her irrational agreement to murder a man that engaged with her far better than any schmuck she involved herself with romantically.

On top of everything, she was now dealing with this third-party propaganda that her father had conspired against her.

A murderous plot to rid her from overseeing the funds of a life insurance policy was the type of storyline associated with true crime documentaries and blockbuster suspense films, but she did not believe the relationship with her father could lead down the dark road to a similar scenario. She was his only child. He looked after her and always checked in to make sure she was okay. He provided for her financially any time she needed additional income to make ends meet, and he helped her in a big way to get the house in the cul de sac following the nasty split from Sierra's father.

The policy payout might stand at a staggering two million but Liam had so much in savings that he didn't need to weave some perilous formula to replace her name on the trust.

Plus he was the one who pushed to make Sierra the beneficiary in the first place because he believed the innocence of a child would put the inheritance to good use at the right age.

Casper's assertion wasn't just upsetting and implausible, but it also utterly eradicated what she previously debated as being a reposeful two night getaway from ordinary responsibilities.

She rolled on her back and looked at the ceiling darkening with the slow depletion of exterior light shining through the unblinded window. She wasn't sure how long she'd been in the room but it felt like forever and a day already. Plenty of time must have passed since half the room surrendered to shade. While it was likely a few hours away from her usual bedtime, she was surprisingly tired from acute boredom. There was no TV in the bedroom. No radio. She didn't have her phone since Elliot violently attacked, leaving everything behind except her.

Casper hadn't checked on her, which was probably best for her peace of mind because she was on edge and felt that just a glimpse of him could provoke a negative reaction.

Lowering her prematurely somnolent and rightfully enraged self under the wool blanket, she closed her eyes with hope that she'd mostly sleep off the majority of her time spent here.

All of her emotional burdens rotated slowly around her consciousness sinking deep into a darkness more distant than the form she presently occupied.

CHAPTER ELEVEN

Hundreds of treetops woven together with lush greenery dimmed the dead leaf blanketed underbelly of the wilderness. Death upon the ground was crisp; if an acorn dropped, then its sudden burial might spread nature's mournful disturbance outwards in a circumference of several feet. The slightest sound caused by anything would likely be magnified in this atmosphere holding an eerily silent similarity to a cemetery.

Standing behind the stout trunk of an oak tree was a short and slim plain Jane. She appeared to be undergoing an identity crisis by presenting the unusual blend of brat smothered in tomboy; knee slit denim leggings, basic gray T-shirt with **ARMY** pressed in black lettering across the chest, and hair slung back in a ponytail. Her pale, freckled face lacked makeup which would have shrouded such characteristics she considered were natural defects. There was of course no hope that any cosmetic touch up could enhance her visage in this stifling humidity that quickly greased her skin with sweat. The only feminine trait was butterfly earrings in double piercings in her ears.

Remaining silent, as though to avoid detection, she eased her head halfway from behind the tree and scouted her right side surroundings with just one eye. Beside a tree fairly larger than all the others around her, and approximately sixty feet across from her hiding place, she saw another individual accompanying her in the woodland. He stood with his back to the side of the tree, compacting himself in a way to try and prevent making his shoulders visible beyond the width of bark secreting him. Regrettably, one disadvantage with potential to scream his whereabouts was the clothes he showed up wearing; basic white T-shirt, orange mesh shorts, and white sneakers. He could be the most nonverbally stealth person between them but the colors upon him said everything.

She didn't know anything about the boy. Honestly, she met him for the first time about an hour ago. Their parents came together for a small social occasion and dragged them into the event. He told her his name during the initial introduction but she deemed the information to be unimportant and forgot it shortly after. He also attempted shaking hands but she was too antisocial to welcome the offer.

A loud, constant crunching of dead leaves approached their position.

"I know y'all didn't go far!" shrieked a young male voice. "Y'all don't know this area like I do! I know all the spots!"

The bratty tomboy watched the kid ahead of her and almost burst out laughing. He was tense, pressing his eyes shut, and working his lips like he was talking to himself without actually making a sound. Her immediate thought was that he was praying not to be discovered. She pulled her head back behind the tree and continued holding one hand over her mouth. She couldn't risk looking at him for another second because that built up potential burst of laughter was on the verge of spilling forward and giving away her position.

"I bet y'all are together, feeling up on each other and God knows what else!" the approaching voice suggested, trying to provoke a verbal response.

Bratty tomboy knew the deal and she refrained from falling for the trick.

The kid across from her must have been clever too, because he stayed quiet also.

"Can't hide forever!" the voice confessed.

Now, more than ever, she recognized how close it was to her.

The fast shuffling of leaves was so near that she believed it had taken place on the opposite side of the tree from where she was standing.

"Gotcha!" the voice blared excitedly.

Bratty tomboy held her breath.

She waited.

But nobody emerged from behind either side of the tree.

"It was those fucking shorts, dude! You look like you just broke out of prison!" the voice confirmed, cackling.

"Yeah, I figured they'd give me away! Couldn't find a big enough area to cover myself!" mouthed the boy that had been hiding next to the tree.

"She with you?" asked the second boy.

"Nah," replied the kid in the orange shorts, stepping away from the tree.

The second boy eyed all around their noiseless surroundings. "Then where is she?"

She didn't see but the boy in the orange shorts pointed his finger in her direction. The second boy looked at the tree directly beside him. This tree was the same one brought to his attention. He was so close that he reached out and touched the trunk without taking a step.

"Boo!" he yelled, after leaning over and peering behind it.

She jumped when he appeared unexpectedly.

"Shit," she complained, finally lowering her hand from her mouth.

Her near giggle disintegrated abruptly at the moment she was discovered. Evidently she no longer found humor in fun and games. Maybe she was exhibiting symptoms of being a sore loser for getting tracked down, because she was positive that not anyone could chance upon her. After letting out a quiet growl followed by a haughty sigh, she rolled over sideways and revealed her wholesome self to them before stepping away from the tree.

"Thought I'd found the perfect spot," she grumbled.

The boy that found her hiding place laughed and pointed at the one who ratted her out. "Homeboy here gave you up."

She rolled her eyes at the boy in the orange shorts. "Did your father not tell you it's never a good idea to snitch?"

He shrugged and gave a brief apologetic expression. "I'm sorry. I didn't think he'd find me that quick. It caught me off guard and I didn't know what to say."

"You could've not said anything," she snapped back.

The boy that hunted them stepped beside her. "She

is right. You should've kept your damn mouth shut."

"Oh, so y'all going to gang up on me now?" whined the tattletale.

She glanced at the boy next to her before stepping aside, reclaiming the distance previously between them. This gesture was obviously disapproval toward him for impeding the comfort of her personal space.

"How old are you guys anyway?" he asked, glimpsing at each of them.

"Fifteen," replied the kid in the orange shorts.

Both boys looked at their female companion since she failed to provide an answer.

"What about you, little girl?" asked the one closest to her.

"You'd best not call me little girl," she warned him sternly. "My name's Shei, and I advise that you refer to me by it."

"Ooooh!" he sounded out sarcastically, raising both hands and shaking them with a ridiculous amount of pretend fear. "Okay, Shei. I'll ask again. How old are you?"

"Thirteen," she replied.

The boy giggled. "Oh, wow! You're like an eighth grader or something. No wonder I don't know you."

"How old are you?" asked the second male, looking up to him.

"I'm seventeen," the kid answered proudly.

"You a senior?" Shei inquired, browsing to the top of his natural height towering over her.

He smirked. "Hell no. I quit that shit. Don't need school to get me anywhere."

Her eyes became well rounded. "How did you pull

that off? I'm surprised your dad didn't kill you."

"Oh, he wasn't happy about it. Threatened to ship me off to boarding school but my mom wasn't having any of that. Now he treats me like some reject who's thrown their life away," he unloaded.

His admittance to being a bad boy seemed to instantly mesmerize her because she couldn't take her eyes off him. She presumed him to be a little older before he stated the fact. Height was one indication but the primary takeaway was the depth of maturity in his tone. He had surpassed the crackly squeak associated with the transition from childhood.

The interesting element pertaining to all the trouble surrounding him was the fact that he didn't resemble what she suspected a deadbeat might look like. This young man was wearing expensive brand name athletic shoes, brown cargo shorts, and black polo shirt with a three button collar. Staying true to the rebel persona, only one button was fastened. If Shei didn't know anything about his father, then she may have taken him for a preacher's son.

"Do either of you take risks?" he inquired, digging inside one of his shorts pockets.

"Guess it depends," said the younger boy. "My dad does everything by the book, so I try not to do anything that'll get me in serious trouble. He can be a real asshole."

"Your dad's a cunt," joked the eldest kid.

"Hey, now! What the hell?!" squalled the less unruly male.

The troublesome teen extended his long, lanky arm and lightly punched the boy's shoulder. "Get over it, bro. You might be the new kid in town but you've got to get used to catching some heat. One thing you'll learn around here is how all of us like to fuck with each other."

Shei tried everything not to smile but understood it was impossible to completely rid. The troublemaker was correct - kids and bullying were more compatible than intimacy between any two parents. Of course, she didn't receive negative attention like most kids did. Being a prosecuting attorney's daughter had its perks, but there did exist some minor disadvantages. A particular constituent was the badmouthing by fellow classmates that she, herself, unintentionally heard. Minding her own business in one of the women's restroom stalls, she overheard a couple of girls mention her by other names; spoon fed hoochie, attention whore, and rich bitch - just to name a few. However, no one ever said such derogative things to her face because everyone feared that she was the special privileged kind of girl that would go at someone, swinging her fists, and not be subjected to consequences.

The seventeen year old pulled a lighter and pack of cigarettes from his pocket.

Shei wasn't necessarily thrilled with the idea of puffing a cigarette because she had never tried or thought about tasting one, but her eagerness to impress the eldest teen elevated curiosity so much that she bypassed feeling peer pressure.

"Umm- Nope! Not doing it!" exclaimed the younger boy. "Count me out."

"Pussy," stated the older teen, laughing.

"Pussy? Our parents would smell that shit all over us," defended the apparent scaredy-cat.

"We're outside, dumbass . They're not going to

notice. Besides, we're at a cookout; that funky grill smoke will mask everything," assured the seventeen year old, before taking one cigarette from the pack and lighting it.

He inhaled a quick breath from the filter and then exhaled smoke when reaching the cigarette in front of the boy.

"No way. I said I'm not taking any part in this," the fifteen year old refused, taking a few steps away to prevent the odor from absorbing into his shirt.

"I'll do it!" Shei hailed, reaching out to accept without having it offered. The wish to see him interested in her decimated underlying dread by not allowing it to spill within her voice.

"All right!" lauded the oldest teen, turning and handing her the cigarette.

Since it was her first time, she took a brief drag of the filter.

The seventeen year old glanced back at their party pooper sidekick. "She's got larger balls than you do."

"Y'all are stupid," mouthed the fifteen year old.

Smoke coursing down her throat left a conflagrant sensation in her esophagus and soon her lungs felt like they were on fire. Discomfort caused her to exhale but the effort was complicated by her coughing the smoke out. The cigarette was the worst thing she'd ever tasted. She realized that her face had crumpled with revulsion but it must not have been too big of a deal because neither boy remarked.

A woman's voice called out from someplace distant, "Dillon!"

"Shei!" followed a man's voice.

"Shit. Quick, give it to me," rushed the older teen.

She simply let go since he reached and practically pried her fingers apart to forcibly claim the cigarette. He took two long draws off it, refusing to expel the first breath before taking the second. Then he tossed the remaining half on the ground and rubbed it into the dirt beneath his shoe.

"Guess they're ready," he mentioned, having thick gusts of smoke roll off his words.

"Thank God. I'm starving," said the younger boy.

The seventeen year old gave him a hard look. "Keep your mouth shut. You didn't see anything."

The boy slipped both hands into the pockets of his orange shorts, and nodded. "Okay. I didn't see anything. It's cool. I get it."

"If you go as far as to even give a vague hint, then I will find you when you're alone and stomp your ass," warned the eldest teen.

They wandered together through a short distance of woodland and stumbled upon a large clearing. Shei got a pleasant up close view of the marvelous two-story cabin style retreat when arriving, but a renewed visual caused her to adore the place with awe all over again. She saw Alfonso Reyes standing on the front of the large deck that wrapped completely around the house. He was grinning and swaying his head while holding a metal spatula in one hand and a brown glass beer bottle in the other. She heard the other adults laughing and talking but couldn't see them. Rolling her eyes at their behavior, she disliked knowing things were only going to get worse because this was just the beginning.

Shei led the boys to the staggering fleet of stairs ahead of three vehicles parked in the broad gravel driveway.

"Almost time to eat, sweetheart," stated Priscella Rivera, after seeing her daughter's head rise above the handrail near the top of the steps.

Shei reached the porch and the boys trailed indirectly. She found her mother sitting in a plastic chair with her back to the balusters in the deck railing. Next to her was a round glass top patio table. The right side pressed flush against the railing and the left side was accompanied by a chair that seated a woman whom she didn't know. In fact, Shei had never seen the lady until today. She believed this woman was the mother of the boy in the orange shorts. Her father never spoke personally about the new family; therefore, she didn't know any of their names. On the opposite end of the table sat Alfonso's wife. Shei thought her name was Grace but she wasn't too sure because the only person here that her father talked highly about was Alfonso. Every time Dillon was mentioned, he was referred to as *that boy*, and Grace was commonly labeled *his wife*. If she did know anything else about them, then she learned it so long ago that it became suppressed over time.

"Are you boys ready to eat?" asked the unnamed woman.

"Yep," Dillon replied, stepping ahead of Shei.

"All Dillon wants to do is eat," Grace confirmed, swatting at a fly buzzing beside her head. Presumably she frightened the pest away because she brought her hand back down on her leg. Then she smiled, giggling briefly. "He'd eat the ass out of a hog if you put it in front of him."

The women laughed.

Shei didn't think the joke was funny and considered

their reaction to be ludicrously exaggerated.

Dillon wasn't laughing either. He crossed the deck, leaving Shei and the other boy standing away from everyone. "Real funny, mom," he pitched along the way.

"Best be the only ass he eats. Kid's got another year to go before he can start thinking about anything else," Alfonso blurted out, using the spatula to pick up a thoroughly cooked hamburger patty off the grill and drop it over onto a paper plate with other patties and hotdog wieners on the side table attachment.

"Alfonso!" Liam shrieked, sitting in a plastic patio chair alongside the third father, only a few feet from the grill butted against a partition of log siding between two massive windows providing a clear view inside the home. "You can't say things like that; my daughter's here."

Alfonso shrugged. "Oh, big deal. They hear all sorts of garbage in school. I'm sure anything we could say wouldn't come close."

"I second that," said the father newest to the group. "They're pushing to teach family life education to elementary students. For us, it was what, tenth or eleventh grade?"

Dillon stepped next to his father and stole a wiener from the plate. One bite and he depleted it to hold just a half.

"Dammit, Dillon! I didn't fix extra for you to come poke your fingers through," Alfonso complained.

"Sorry. I'm hungry," Dillon replied, chewing.

"It's not ass you're going to have to worry about," mentioned the unnamed man.

Everyone - except Dillon and Shei - cackled.

Dillon crammed the remaining chunk of wiener inside his mouth before pointing at the guy that made the comment. "Screw you, man."

"Dillon!" Alfonso snapped. "Mind your manners."

Escaping the adults' nonsense roguery, Shei looked at the huge left window and was immediately intimidated while peering inside the house. Just the estimated value of the materialistic amenities caused her to feel like her parents were raising her in poverty, and that idea was far from the truth. The Rivera's were a prosperous family, living in one of Roanoke's flourishing taintless neighborhoods, and income didn't strain them the way it did most families. But the Reyes' summer home was unlike anything she'd ever seen.

Dark leather furniture dressed the living quarters and none of it resembled easily obtainable, thinly padded cheap stuff. A beautiful bearskin rug stretched across the hardwood floor and next to it stood an engaging fireplace.

All she could really make out in the distant scenery was stainless steel kitchen appliances; basically just the refrigerator and an oven embedded in the wall. Her view of everything else was obstructed by an island standing between the living room and kitchen. Above the island, she saw a portion of the second floor; two doors beyond a bannister facing the living room below.

During the time she admired the interior, everyone around her went eerily mute. She didn't know when their conversation stopped or why they quit joking because she had been too absorbed in the incredible beauty of the place. She looked toward the grill but, surprisingly, it was no longer there. Strangely, the men were gone too. Even

Dillon had vanished.

Somewhat disturbed by them leaving her, Shei spun around and confronted the rest of the deck. Her mother and both women had disappeared, along with the table and chairs. The boy in the orange shorts was missing too.

Suddenly she realized the potent aroma of cookout was absent from the air.

A profoundly depressing sense of abandonment overwhelmed her, and was accompanied by confusion. It was bizarre how everyone managed to evaporate and she did not hear them leave. Certainly, they couldn't have gone far; there was nowhere for them to go. The wilderness stretched for miles. One direction was identical to the next and getting lost would be unchallenging.

"Mom?!" she called out anxiously.

Soundlessness was the response provided by nature.

"Dad?!"

Still nothing.

Shei walked to the deck railing where the table previously stood and what she discovered abruptly saturated her with fear. There were no vehicles in the parking lot. Confusedness plagued her mind. Where did everyone go? How did they take off without her knowledge, and why did they leave her behind? She had a dozen questions but not one answer.

An ominous darkness consumed the sun and every visible stretch of blue in the sky. Surrounding treetops - chock-full of vegetation - brushed together and hissed with no wind present to guide them. Lastly, she felt an intangible force hold her stationary, as if something with detrimental intent wanted her suffering seclusion in every way possible.

Darkness bled between distant trees.

Eventually, all the woodland succumbed to the wave of impenetrable pitch-black sliding toward the cabin.

Shei held her breath.

Had no choice but to witness herself get devoured by that endless gulf of murk.

The isolation it provided struck her worse than the moment she recognized everyone disappeared. Her unpleasant evening with childish adults and two boys she honestly didn't know transformed into a memory she wished to relive.

Towed deep inside the voluminous discontinuity of existence, she surrendered her subsistence dissipating in a thousand directions of illimitable nothingness.

CHAPTER TWELVE

Shei bolted upright.

She woke up panicked, gasping for breath - glazed with sweat.

She had pulled away from a nightmare that also functioned as a memory pertaining to a point in her life that she hadn't reflected in recent years. There was good reason she'd been summoned to recapture that particular event; it reacquainted her with the unfamiliar. She wasn't being held at some random residence. Shei knew this place, although she'd forgotten until having that wretched dream.

Vaguely capable of seeing her surroundings, she rushed off the bed in a panic and made a dash for the door. The mystification encircling her circumstance intensified. Fleeing the room, she hurried to the door of the supposed bedroom beside her, thinking Casper might be able to provide details which may help her understand things clearly.

"Hey!" she squawked, barging upon another dimly lit room.

The layout of the bedroom was identical to the one she stormed away from. Casper laid on the full size bed with a checkerboard pattern wool blanket pulled over him, in front of a large, curtainless half moon shaped window. The majority of moonlight cast into the room fell across the bed, making him the only thing she could really distinguish while darkness loitered all around.

Her brazen entrance failed to rouse him. Or make him flench. Instead of wasting her effort by yelling at him again, she approached the bed. She grabbed his arm outside the blanket and immediately felt intimidated by how small her hands appeared against his husky bicep. She knew he was a stout man - but damn - the solidity beneath his skin was impressive. For the moment, all she could do was squeeze his arm, as if temporarily derailed from comprehending her earliest intent.

She shook him eventually, but he didn't budge.

"I know where we are!" she voiced anyway.

Her words did nothing but fall on deaf ears.

She shook him once more, harder this time.

He jerked his arm back and she let go. Casper rolled on his back, opening his eyes and squinting straightaway. He reached up while trying to get a visual of what was going on and scrubbed the sleep from his eyes. Then he dragged himself upright, allowing the blanket to drop off his large, shirtless chest.

"What are you doing?" he asked groggily.

She swayed her hands with anxiety while explaining, "It's going to sound crazy but I know this place. I came here with my parents for a cookout a long time ago. This is his place. Judge Reyes' summer house."

"I know where we are. I thought you knew already," he admitted.

"Why would they bring me here?" she asked, overlooking his comment. "It doesn't make sense. I don't understand what Alfonso has to do with any of this."

Casper expired a wearisome breath. "You still don't get it, do you?"

"Get what?" she questioned fanatically.

"Judge Reyes is just as much a part of this as your father. With you out of the way, your father will have the means necessary to contest the trust, and who does he have that will sign off on it? Judge Alfonso Reyes. I'm sure he was promised a cut from the payout like I've been. You've got to believe what I'm saying is true. Reyes will do anything if he knows he can benefit. They like to make you think they're running a clean system, but it's crooked. Everything about it is," he addressed.

She stayed silent. She didn't know what to think or how to respond to his admission. Of course she didn't want to believe any of this was true, but it did make sense. There were no loose ends that voided how it all could be tied together. No part of his claim sounded too far-fetched.

"Alfonso has known me for over half my life. He's never done anything dirty that I know of," she said, struggling not to accept the astounding revelation.

Casper reached down and tapped the narrow space between him and the edge of the mattress. "Sit," he encouraged.

She discourteously resisted.

"It's okay, I don't bite," he stated.

She remained quiet while taking her place beside him. He crossed his arms against his thick pectorals, as though passing the idea on to her that she didn't have anything to worry about with them being so close to each other on the bed.

"Alfonso used to be an outstanding guy. He'd help

anyone that truly needed assistance. Didn't matter if it was someone he knew or a stranger on the streets. When he and Grace divorced, then he made a turn for the worse. He started gambling, cutting deals with the same people he sentenced, and doing all kinds of shady shit that's not common for a man in his position. Maybe you did know him years back, but he isn't someone you can trust anymore," Casper explained.

Shei scratched her nose. "How do you know so much about him?"

"He had a son named Dillon. He and I used to run around together. We got ourselves in trouble more than anything," he replied.

She nodded. "I remember that kid. The first time I met him was here, when our parents had a get together one summer. Whatever happened to him?"

Casper frowned. "He committed suicide."

"Oh my god. That's horrible," she gasped.

"Yeah. It's unfortunate,' he spoke quietly.

She caught herself staring at his arms and quickly withdrew from admiring his masculinity. "If they hired you to take care of the job for them, then why aren't you still going along with the plan?"

"Because it was never my idea to harm you in the first place," he revealed.

"So what was your plan?" she inquired.

"Remember the case that involved me supposedly killing a child during a drunk driving incident?" he asked.

"Yeah," she answered swiftly. "Who doesn't know? It was broadcast on every news station there is."

"Truth is I didn't kill the kid. I wasn't the one

driving that night. Dillon was behind the wheel. We weren't paying attention to the road because we were too busy fucking around and being stupid. Neither of us saw the girl riding her bicycle on the sidewalk. If I did, then I would have jerked the wheel and caused us to run off the road, striking a light pole instead."

"How did you get convicted if you weren't driving?" she questioned.

He sighed. "Because Alfonso and your father are real pricks. They got Dillon to lie and say I was driving just to protect the reputation of the family name. I thought I had a good lawyer to beat the charge but your father got to him and everything went downhill from there. I didn't stand a chance. Dillon couldn't bear living with the fact he was responsible but allowed me to take the fall, so he put a gun to his head and that's all she wrote."

"I'm sorry," she said, before reaching and grabbing his closest arm which resulted in him unfolding both of them from shielding his chest. She laid his arm on his lap outside the blanket and slid her fingers down his wrist to grasp his hand gently.

"If they made you the fall guy for a crime you didn't commit, then why are you dealing with them now?" she asked.

He scraped his thumb over the back of her hand. "Your father offered me fifteen grand and the opportunity to have my record cleared. What they don't know is that Dillon left behind all the evidence to have my conviction overturned. He kept everything in a diary that Alfonso locked up before his suicide. I managed to get in and get it a while back. He's not mentioned anything, so I don't think he has checked to find it missing."

Shei shook her head. "Wait a second. I'm confused. You're saying my father paid you fifteen thousand dollars to murder me?"

He leaned off the pillow and headboard. "I wasn't lying to you at dinner when I said he's willing to give me fifteen grand. And no, he's not paid me yet. His idea is to pay off everyone when he takes on overseeing your daughter's account."

"I think I'm going to be sick," she mentioned, attempting to pull her hand away but he wouldn't let go. "I can't believe he would do something like this. I mean what kind of man looks after his daughter and then one day decides to have her offed in cold blood?"

"A man that really isn't much of a father," he replied.

"He'll not get away with this. He can't," she uttered dishearteningly.

Without letting go of her hand, he reached up and placed his other one on her slim shoulder. "They're not going to get away with anything. Nothing is going to happen to you. I'll not let it."

"I've been betrayed," she rattled quietly. "I can't trust anyone, really."

Casper huffed. "Don't say that. I'm sure there are plenty of people that would look out for your best interest. You just can't trust the ones you thought were closest to you."

She tried pulling her hand free again, but he still didn't let go. "I don't know what to do now," she stressed.

He squeezed her slender shoulder. "You don't have

to do anything. Let's get through these nights and I'll figure out what to do. I promise that no one is going to lay a hand on you."

She scanned the darkness around them briefly. Even the night haunted her with uncertainty. Every formidable revelation caused constant discomfort in her comprehension of reality. If everything he told her was true, then she'd been groomed and doublecrossed since her mother's passing. All acts of concern perpetrated by her father were strategically conducted.

"I'm not trying to sound weird but is it possible I can sleep in here? I don't think I'd feel comfortable being alone because now I feel like I've got to watch my back every time I turn around. No offense," she spoke quietly.

Finally, he released her hand and scooted across on the opposite side of the bed. "Sure. There's plenty of room for you to have your own space."

She pulled the blanket down. "No funny stuff, mister. I'm only doing this to feel safe having someone next to me."

"Nothing crossed my mind," he replied, sliding down on the bed and fluffing the pillow beneath his head.

She pulled the blanket over her and relinquished her angst to the relaxing heat provided by him laying in the exact spot recently. The bed was cozy, and his presence consoled her security. She closed her eyes and turned her head to the side facing away from him. Shortly afterwards her body followed with her back to him.

"How did you know where to find the diary?" she inquired.

He slipped one hand between the pillow and back of

his head while resting the other on his chest outside the blanket. "I used to hang with Dillon a lot at their house. Alfonso wasn't very sneaky about where he placed things of importance. Guess he didn't expect me knowing would come back to bite him one day."

She rotated her right shoulder before tugging the blanket under the bottom of her face. "What are you going to do?"

"Like I originally intended. Fifteen grand is nothing compared to the lawsuit I can bring against them. Plus I'd have charges filed against them and likely have their jobs," he stated.

Eventually, they laid silently within the moonlight pressing the length of the bed. The entire cabin was quiet, making the night eerily peaceful. Unable to sleep, Casper peered straight up at the dark ceiling. He thought about Shei's predicament; how discouraging it truly might be for her having no one in life that she could positively trust. It was a brutal insult that everything she was informed to do was actually arranged against her. He believed if he had stepped into this situation with the mindset to follow instructions, then he wouldn't have the desire to execute those orders in the end. She was too generous, and vulnerable. He couldn't willfully take the life of someone undeserving of such tragedy. He'd been around her for too long and was enjoying her company.

Shei wanted to sleep but feared she'd find herself sinking inside another nightmare. She didn't want to relive past experiences because they had potential to wreak havoc on her mental state, especially with her mother playing a role in those occurrences. Coping with loss was difficult enough without the need of some painful reminder showing how precious her mother was in life. Having Casper near did eliminate loneliness, but he could not cure all of her emotional ailments.

"Not to sound weird but do you think you can hold me?" she asked.

One of his brows raised when he glanced at her beside him without turning his head. "Uh- Are you sure?"

"Yes," she replied, keeping her eyes closed. "It might help if I feel you're here rather than just knowing. Keep your hands out of the blanket of course."

"Sure. I mean if it helps, then I've got no problem with it," he said, creating a lot of commotion by shaking the mattress when turning on his side and scooting toward her.

She nearly groaned when his arm came down from behind and crushed her stomach. Instead of embracing her gently, like she imagined a gentleman would do, he landed on top of her hard, as if he was an opponent trying to grapple her in a WWE event. Then he pulled her toward him aggressively, and she didn't halt until her back slammed his chest.

"Good God. How long has it been since you've had a woman?" she asked, discharging a quick gust of respiratory distress while assembling everything that just happened.

"Two - Two and a half years. Why?" he inquired.

"It's kind of noticeable," she answered, wriggling to find comfort in being constricted.

"Well, when you're someone like me with a manslaughter conviction attached to your name, you forget how you're supposed to handle people because you've grown used to your past pushing everyone away," he admitted.

"Did you tell them you didn't do it?" she asked straightaway.

"Yeah, but they chose to believe in the system. People think a conviction guarantees you did the crime. They don't understand the crooked politics amongst attorneys. How both sides cut a deal to seal your fate," he responded.

She slid the back of her head toward him and squirmed once more, finally making herself cozy. "Maybe one day," she uttered, smiling halfway.

"No. I gave up on that hope a long time ago," he mentioned.

Some time passed and Shei still hadn't fallen asleep. She was close though; caught on the verge of grogginess becoming full blown nirvana. She wasn't afraid of wandering into whatever dreamscape since Casper's hold exiled that dread. Also, she enjoyed the comfort he provided. Like him, it had been a while since she felt the closeness of another person. She missed having physical support, although she wished to forget the last individual she allowed to half-ass console her. Deepening her mind's submission, she drifted peacefully into dark oblivion.

Casper readjusted his head when her hair began tickling his face, and he lightened his grip. He couldn't tell Shei, but it had been more than two and a half years since he'd given affection to anyone. Actually, if his memory was correct, then he hadn't touched a woman for five years. He tried involving himself with a few women following his last short term relationship but nothing ever went past casual talking. They seemed interested in learning more about him until he divulged his involvement with a child's death, because then they ghosted his calls and texts.

He sympathized with Shei for the appalling secrets she learned in one day.

She really didn't know the designed outcome of her association.

Tightening his grip on her again, and pressing the side of his face on the back of her head, Casper repeatedly paid close attention to every detail of their moment together - memorizing the sensual satisfactions, in the event they were his last.

CHAPTER THIRTEEN

Elliot sat in a scruffy recliner against the wood paneled wall, watching a late night talk show on his forty-two inch television which wasn't in the best working condition. There was a large jagged crack in the screen and around it spread a thin mass of darkness lacking even the faintest trace of color projection. It had been that way for several months and served as a constant eyesore to him. He didn't know what happened precisely, but remembered turning violently aggressive during an intoxicant fueled argument. Apparently, he got pissed off enough to throw something and caught the television in his rage.

With a party size bag of unsalted potato chips catering to his nighttime munchies, he held a half drank twenty-four ounce bottle of lukewarm beer which he was using to rinse the soggy residual clumped on his teeth after chewing. Instead of licking the oil coating off his fingers, he swiped them on the arm cushion and streaked the material with five long stains.

Beside the chair stood an end table with the television remote, glass weed pipe, prescription pill bottle, and an ashtray littered with a mix of brown and white filters. On the other side of the table sat a woman in a different color recliner. She held a burning white cigarette in one hand and her cell phone with the other. Uninterested in the television show, she stared at the phone and inquisitively scrolled through social media.

Her scrawny appearance implied that she wasn't in the best health. Someone may look at her and assume she was anywhere between one hundred five and one hundred fifteen pounds, and they might be right. Her skin was dark, wrinkled, and leathery - all supporting indications that years worth of inhaling ingredients in a filter had taken a devastating toll on her skin care. Dark gray rings circled her deep-set green eyes. Her frizzy medium length light brown hair was sprinkled with singular white strands scattered all around.

"Whatcha getting into tomorrow?" Elliot asked, after taking a quick swig from the bottle.

She didn't answer. All she did was continue scrolling through the social feed on her phone.

"I asked you a question, woman!" he snapped.

"I gotta take Jimmy to the dentist in the morning. He's gotta have a damn tooth filled. Boy's been eating too much crap that ain't good for him. Might stop for some groceries when we get done, then gotta do laundry," she replied nervously. In fact, she became so anxious that her head trembled while speaking.

"Has he went and got his learner's yet?" he asked.

She shook her head but Elliot didn't see since he was focused on the television. "Nah. He hasn't mentioned it either. I think he's afraid to get behind the wheel," she stated.

"Well, he's gonna have to get over that. Can't be relying on you to take him everywhere all the time. You ain't gonna be around forever," he mentioned.

"Yeah. He'll get it one day," she spluttered.

He shoved a handful of chips inside his mouth and chewed them down to a thick paste before taking a drink to make swallowing less difficult. "Speaking of not always being around… I've got an important job tomorrow. I mean huge. The paycheck isn't life changing but it'll be enough for a new start."

Finally, she peeled her eyes away from the phone and looked at him facing the television. "Are you dealing shit again? You better not be, Elliot. You're looking at hard time for that last bust already."

He chuckled. "Naw. I ain't selling nothing, and I ain't delivering nothing either. I was just asked to do a job and promised compensation, that's all. I ain't moving no product when my face is on the watch list of every police department in the state."

"Then what do you got to do?" she asked.

"It's best if I don't provide details. Let me just say it's serious business. Not everybody is cut out for it," he remarked.

She went back to browsing on her phone. "As long as I don't get a call from you in jail, then it ain't none of my concern."

"Ain't gotta worry about jail. I'm walking after this," he assured.

"Better keep your nose clean. You've about used up nine lives," she announced.

He raised the bottle and eyeballed how much alcohol remained. Maybe there was enough for a few drinks. Or one decent chug. However he decided to consume this last portion, it certainly wasn't going to end in satisfaction. Elliot wanted to tie on a good buzz but he still wasn't feeling any effects three beers later, despite them being twenty-four ounce bottles. He drank daily for a number of years that he built a high tolerance. Turning the bottle up, he chose to finish it all at once.

Having no more to drink, he picked up the bag of chips and placed it on the end table before standing with the bottle in one hand. "You've gotta be ready to go in a couple months. Jimmy too."

"What do we have to be ready for?" she asked, without providing her undivided attention.

He crossed the living room, swinging the bottle by his side. "You're gonna pack your shit and come with me. We're getting the hell outta this godforsaken place. I'm thinking we can start fresh in New Mexico. Nevada, maybe. Anywhere far from here, where I can walk in someplace and not get called by name."

"Elliot, there ain't nothing out there for me and Jimmy. He's just got a few years and then he'll be out on his own. We can't go anywhere he ain't got no friends," she informed.

"That boy's just a kid. He's got plenty of years in him to make new friends. Would be the same if y'all stayed here and he graduated. He'd have to make friends all over again in the real world, so don't feed me bullshit that he ain't gonna have nobody," he said, tossing the bottle amongst others inside the half full thirty-two gallon trash can in the kitchen.

He glanced on the table and saw three small lines of white powder on the red cover of a notebook. Beside it was a two inch piece of plastic straw, likely used to sniff the aligned substance.

"Do you want any more of this?" he asked, bypassing the temptation.

"Any more of what?" she inquired.

"This skag," he specified.

"Nah. I think I've had enough. I've gotta watch myself with that stuff. Wouldn't take much to lay me up in the ER," she said.

"Oh, Darlene. You've gotta stop being such a pussy," he stated.

"Damn you, Elliot; I ain't no pussy! I overdosed once, and that was some scary shit! It aint' no joke," she retaliated, taking offense to his remark.

Disregarding the well-being of others was all that he knew, and so he laughed at her rejection while opening the refrigerator and snatching another large bottle off the second shelf. Shutting the door, he unscrewed the cap before turning and firing a perfect shot into the trash can across the room. Then he turned the bottle up and chugged. After lowering it, he saw that he had reduced the beverage below the top of the label.

"You're sure you're good?" he asked, walking to the table and setting the bottle down.

"Hell yeah, I'm sure!" she snapped irritably.

He bent over, picking up the straw. He stuck one end inside his nostril and touched the other against the notebook. Slowly, he inhaled an entire line. Then he dropped the straw and stood upright. Picking up the bottle, he sniffed deeply to drag the heroin down his throat after clearing his nasal cavity. It didn't numb his esophagus the way past cocaine use did but the taste was second best, no doubt. This batch was superior to any cut he'd tasted in months.

He smiled. "I might like you to refuse often. Leaves more for me."

Darlene may have heard his boast but she didn't have anything to say.

He stepped in the vast space connecting both rooms. The front of his feet stood upon the living room carpet and the back of them pressed linoleum. He glanced at Darlene sitting across from his right side while rearing his head just slightly and taking a guzzle from the bottle. She wasn't his true love interest but would have to do, since his main attraction was unavailable; therefore, he actually had no emotional ties with this leather skin shrine of bones.

The woman that caught his eye was an attorney who defended him on a narcotics possession charge six years ago. She didn't beat the case, however, she certainly won him over. That curly blonde hair and those refulgent green eyes mesmerized him the first time he saw her. He remembered her name was Layla but he couldn't recall the last name. The only reason he recollected her first name was because it sounded like it should belong to a stripper. She definitely had sublimity if she ever wanted to woo men by having them toss dollar bills while she worked the stage.

He didn't know if she was married and the possibility didn't really matter. All that concerned him was that she was a pleasant piece of work to admire, and she was incredibly polite. At least, that appeared to be the case during their few interactions. Layla didn't prevent him from getting locked up all those years ago but he'd hire her once more just to see her again.

Darlene did the exact opposite for him. There was nothing about her that he kept his eyes on for long periods of time. Truthfully, the nights she came over and they had sex, one of two things happened - Eilliot would turn off the light or shut his eyes. Everything worked out for the best if he couldn't see her and pretended that she was someone else. He made the mistake of looking at her in the past, several times, and each incident concluded with his performance ending prematurely because one look at her unsightly face euthanized an erection.

The only reason he got involved with her in the first place was for her companionship. She was someone to drink beer with, sniff powder, and shoot the shit. It began with them hanging out and doing just those things, but Elliot had gone for too long without intimacy that Darlene's proximity to him made her functional in suspending the drought.

Meaningless casual sex with someone who'd give him the time of day, that's all it was to him. No emotional attachment, and definitely no having to answer to anyone. Maybe his lack of empathy was the culprit behind him beating the hell out of her half the time. Darlene took so much abuse; most of the time it came in the form of spontaneous fits of rage. She was terrified of him. Fear might be the reason she trembled when speaking to him.

His purpose for wanting to drag her out west involved having someone familiar to speak with and guaranteed sex. He considered the possibility of eventually meeting someone else and decided that if it happened, then he'd kick Darlene and her lazy ass son out of wherever they ended up. Elliot knew he was selfish to plan things based just on what he wanted but he genuinely didn't care. He took pride in Darlene not having any say about what she could do for herself; furthermore, it delighted him knowing that her only choice was going to be to pack her belongings and leave with him - just to allow herself to get verbally degraded and violently assaulted.

He crossed the room, returning to his recliner. "I'd say you've got a minimum of two months before we go anywhere. Gives you plenty of time to pack up, notify the school that Jimmy will no longer be attending, close out your bank account, and put your house on the market. Or you can rent it out. Doesn't matter which."

"I don't see us just up and taking off like you expect," she claimed.

He sat the beer in front of the potato chips on the table. "You're gonna be ready when I say to be. All that you've gotta do is make sure you're prepared, because you know how I get if I've gotta wait on you."

"It ain't that easy putting my house up for sale. I've lived there for twenty-three years. There's a lot of memories in that place," she stated anxiously.

He snapped his head around and studied her scornfully. "Don't give me any lip about it. You'll call the real estate agent and they'll handle everything. Now as far as your memories, fuck 'em - you'll make plenty of new ones where we're going."

She laid the phone on her thigh to hide broadcasting how severely it trembled in her hand. The only thing she could not disguise was her head shivering while she glowered at him. Perhaps she was petrified seeing the way he stared at her, like it was a presentiment of something awful.

"My whole life is here. I can't leave everything because you-"

"Goddamn you, Darlene! You're working my buttons. You know that, right? If I say you're gonna do something, then you're gonna start on it tomorrow. End of discussion," he scolded her.

She leaned forward before reaching out and crushing the remaining portion of cigarette in the ashtray. Then she pulled the phone to her side and stood. Keeping her teary, panic-stricken eyes on him, she began to proceed slowly - as if trying to bide her time until he became calm enough for her to pass without risk of escalating potential conflict.

"Come here," he demanded.

She paused before being able to step in front of him.

The strictness in his voice sliced her dread, making her unsure what to do. She felt the situation would not turn out well if she acknowledged the request. That cold, offset glare in his eyes defined everything she feared to conceive. The presumptive demonic energy that manifested every time they reached a disagreement had surfaced. This particular demeanor wasn't satisfied unless it bruised a rib or darkened the preexisting shade around her eyes. Its savage hunger often left Darlene fearing for her life, because Elliot reacted on impulse and there was never a warning sign about how far he could go to inflict injury.

"Don't make me tell you twice," he warned.

Understanding that his declaration was nothing to take lightly, she treaded carefully with obedience. He lunged forward and snatched her by the arm. She shrieked when he jerked her toward him. Taintless delirium was administered by his clench. She fell on his lap and he let go of her arm, only to take her by the throat and yank her closer. The grip wasn't malicious like she contemplated it would be but mild pressure did cause her to endure difficulty breathing. Since her throat was naturally thin and weak, any amount of tension would create discomfort, unlike what the broader and stronger neck of an average person might feel.

"You got a problem listening to how things are gonna be?" he asked.

She gasped for breath.

Unsurprisingly, he tightened his grip.

The sudden oxygen deprivation caused her to begin choking.

"I'm not hearing anything," he griped.

She grabbed his wrist but failed to lessen the severity of getting strangled. Her view of his vicious expression became blurrily distorted by the thick watery film of fright veiling her eyes. Intuition and past experience made her suspect that something drastic would be the outcome of their interaction. However, she didn't expect to get suffocated since his typical outbursts progressed with her being the recipient of a solid fist.

"No problem," she groaned strenuously.

He smiled, nodded, and pulled away from her throat. "I knew, providing a little effort, you'd see things my way," he mentioned, shoving her off him.

Darlene staggered upright and touched her neck. She sensed shame for not having the backbone to stand against him, but like always, Elliot got his way by not allowing her to make decisions.

He crossed one leg over the other and grabbed the bottle on the table. "What you're gonna do right now is go hop in the shower. I don't wanna smell a rotten crotch when I come to bed later and get up in those guts."

Humiliation was the breaking point of her preservation. She couldn't hold back sobbing any longer, and her entire body struck the peak of shuddering significantly. Obviously, her vulnerabilities were his strengths. Elliot knew this too. He probably wouldn't treat her with savagery if he wasn't aware.

"Do you think I was talking to myself?" he asked, putting the mouth of the bottle to his lips. "Get to it."

Keeping her mouth shut to avoid causing further abuse, she took her low self-esteem and stormed out of the room.

Elliot chuckled prior to taking a drink. Perhaps her final reaction certifiably humbled all aspects of his senseless indecency. Even in her absence, he prolonged disparaging her existence by avowing, "If that damn whore so much as thinks about bailing on me, then I'll take her out and pop her in the woods like the rest of 'em."

CHAPTER FOURTEEN

The melody of birds chirping pried her eyes open. Laying on her back with her face pointing toward the window behind the headboard, Shei squinted and raised one hand above her face to cast shade across her eyes when rolling over on her side and confronting the other half of the bed. She stretched her arm out and rubbed against the mattress before visually recognizing that Casper wasn't lying next to her anymore. She never felt him slide off the bed or noticed that he had pulled away from her at some point. Evidently the comfort from being embraced by him put her in the best sleep she'd gotten in a long while.

She sat up and looked around the room; he was nowhere to be found.

She listened for any sound that might pinpoint where he could be.

Oddly, she heard two voices - a man and woman - somewhere distant outside the bedroom. The male sounded nothing like Casper, and she didn't recognize the female. Paying close attention to their conversation, she overheard them discussing current legal woes within national politics. Could they be hikers traveling through the area who stopped for whatever reason and Casper invited them inside? She didn't know but needed to find out. Since her father was incredibly decisive with his plans, she didn't trust the idea of random travelers just happening to stumble upon the place. Also, she put a lot of trust in Casper but could not be certain that he wasn't involved with a couple of thugs eager to get their hands dirty, regardless of his promise to not let anything happen to her.

She slid off the bed and crept across the room. Fortunately, the door was open and she'd not have to risk making a sound or have anyone downstairs casually glance up and witness it open. The closer she approached the doorway, the louder the unfamiliar voices became.

"It's official! The novel Mask of Dolls by New River Valley horror author Gent Tillbert is set to be adapted for film. Tillbert says the screenplay will be underway within the next several months," the woman stated, shifting the subject away from politics.

"I've actually read a bit of that one," added the male voice.

Shei stepped beyond the doorway and stood upon the narrow balcony overlooking the living room. A quick surge of relief barreled through her when she noticed the television was turned on and the voices she'd been hearing were, in fact, anchors for the morning newscast.

She scanned every direction she was capable of seeing below but didn't spot Casper anywhere.

However, she smelled something.

The inviting aroma ascending from downstairs triggered her to suspect it was the combination of eggs and sausage cooking simultaneously. This exact odor was engraved in her senses because her grandmother prepared breakfast (sausage, eggs, biscuits, gravy) every morning after she spent the night throughout her childhood. Those precious years seemed forever ago but she still clearly recalled how the hot plate was always placed in front of her starving little eyes. One buttermilk biscuit would be pulled apart and separated; on top of it would be a serving of scrambled eggs with a sausage patty broken up and scattered. All of it covered by several large spoonfuls of gravy.

Thinking about her grandmother's cooking made her crave breakfast, although she hadn't eaten much during the mornings for the majority of her adulthood. If she did have something prior to dropping Sierra off at school, then it was quick and easy, like a hot pocket or pop tarts. Her stomach felt that it could go for a decent meal this morning, though, since she abandoned the dinner made for her yesterday evening.

Shei followed the smell down the steps and the first thing she noticed after turning the corner was Casper standing in front of the stovetop, holding a bare glass plate with one hand. She sneaked into the kitchen and tried looking over his shoulder from afar to see if what he prepared was everything she presumed, but his husky width blocked her from glancing past him. Continuing quietly, she made her way around the backside of the island, taking a seat on the stool she claimed yesterday. She humorously watched him go about his business while the jibber jabber of newscasters blasted out of the television across the room behind them.

Casper spun around but then paused any further movement after identifying Shei seated across from him. His surprised expression prompted her to giggle right away.

"Good morning," he greeted, staying in place.

"Good morning to you, too," she said enjoyably.

Slowly, he approached the island, smiling at her along the way. He stopped on the opposite side and reached across to set the plate in front of her. The smell hit her stronger than ever. Admiring what he put together, she was unquestionably impressed with his culinary skills. It certainly wasn't her grandmother's recipe; honestly, this combination he concocted appeared that it might be more appetizing. The scrambled eggs were fluffy with cheese melted over, sausage links were doused in what she thought was barbeque sauce, and the usual buttermilk biscuit was replaced with a dinner roll.

"Wow," she let out, having a hard time pulling away from feeling enthralled. "This looks incredible. I don't mean to intimidate any celebrity chefs out there, but where did you learn to cook?"

He laughed. "Thanks. I had to learn to take care of myself since I've been on my own for the most part."

She dug in with her fingers, peeling a small chunk of egg from the side of the pile. A long string of melted cheese pulled with it and didn't break until the egg reached her lips. She shoved the piece inside her mouth, slurping up the strand of cheese before licking the grease off her fingers. Just one bite into the taste test and her entire upper body wilted forward. Preeminence broadened her eyes. She crossed one hand in front of her mouth; potentially a reaction based on discomfort with him watching her chew.

"Oh my god," she said, immediately after swallowing. "This is so good. Like, really."

"Let me get you a fork," he stated, taking a step backwards and opening the top drawer below the side of the stovetop.

She noticed something peculiar when he came forward with their forks. He was giving her an amusingly cute expression while holding his head cocked at an angle. She waited for him to say something but he didn't. The only thing he did was continue to make that unusual face, and smile.

"What?" she asked, taking one of those forks.

He shook his head without his strange way of looking at her faltering. Then he sat on the stool in front of him. "Nothing. I'm just admiring your bed head. I kinda like it. Looks good on you."

"Oh no!" she gasped, laying the fork beside the plate before raising both hands and touching the sides of her head. She felt the hair on one side was straight and flat but recognized it was puffed out and tangled on the other. "I'm so embarrassed. No one sees me this way, ever."

He glanced down long enough to stab a sausage link with his fork. "Are you saying I should feel honored? Because I will take it as a privilege."

"You should feel grossed out. There's nothing good about this," she expressed, combing her fingers through her hair in an effort to untangle and press it flat against her head.

"Don't be silly. I find you very beautiful. Plus I think you have potential to fill a room with your energy, so you've got a lot going for you," he confessed.

She retrieved the fork and sliced off a small piece of barbeque coated sausage. She didn't know how to respond to the comment because she wasn't accustomed to men making positive remarks. In the real world, she didn't associate with guys often. Negative encounters taught her to live by the motto that all men were pigs, but Casper was beginning to show her a side of the male species that she wasn't aware inhabited them.

"A man would have no idea how lucky he is to be with a girl like you," he added.

Instead of appreciating his politeness, she put the tip of the fork inside her mouth and removed the pierced sausage. Its sensational flavor caught her off guard. He didn't use ordinary barbeque sauce; this was maple honey and it made his rendition of breakfast deliciously irresistible.

"Amazing," she asserted.

He thrust a whole sausage in his mouth, chewed twice, and then tucked it in the pocket of his cheek. "It is pretty decent. I don't know how often Alfonso comes up here but I don't see any problem with us using everything at our disposal. I mean if we don't take advantage of what's provided, then it's likely it'll all go to waste."

"I've noticed you've got no problem making yourself at home," she averred.

Casper raised a forkful of egg over his plate. "Hell no, I don't. They brought us up here, hoping we'd kill each other. Or that one of us would take out the other. I'd say they never imagined we'd get along. I bet they assume we're arguing with each other and keeping our distance. The least they could expect is for us to enjoy all the fine things that have been offered."

"So there's something I've been meaning to ask you. How did you get here? There's no car in the driveway, and I'm pretty sure you didn't walk," she mentioned.

"Do you honestly want to know?" he asked.

"Umm, yeah. If I didn't, then I wouldn't have asked," she replied.

He breathed deeply. "Okay. Truthfully, your dad drove me up here the night before last. He went over everything with me for a second time and told me that you'd show up the following morning."

"What?!" she roared, smacking the plate with the fork. "Really?! The night before I get a bag thrown over my head and slammed on the floor, he's up here chilling and rehearsing whatever arrangement?!"

He readjusted uncomfortably on the stool. Maybe he never anticipated that she'd react aggressively. "He played us both. Everyone who is behind this, set us up. I don't even know what the truth is anymore."

Shei shook her head but didn't give any indication that she was going to throw in the towel over breakfast the way she did with dinner. "We have got to figure out what to do. This is just way too much."

"I suggest that we don't do anything. We wait this out. Then you go your way and I'll go mine. You can say that you wounded me but I got away before you could finish the job. I'll wait a few weeks for everything to die down, then I'll come forward to the public and bust the lid wide open on their operations. I think it sounds like a good idea."

She took a bite of egg while brushing hair on the left side of her face behind her ear. "You make it sound so easy. Like, there aren't going to be repercussions. If they want us dead bad enough, they'll find a way. They will hire some other criminal to track us down, and nobody will know anything because they're powerful enough to make it all disappear."

Casper stabbed another sausage. "Then I'll go public once we get out of here. We'll get to them first and not give 'em time to regroup."

"Easy for you to say. I've got nowhere to go but right back into the arms of the man that put all of this together," she stated.

"Come with me," he encouraged.

"No. I can't do that. I've got to get my daughter. I need to pick her up before I can consider doing anything," she stressed.

"How about I-"

"Oh shit!" she spontaneously interrupted. Uninhibited terror purged normality from her eyes. "We've been assigned to eliminate each other. If one of us was successful, then that still leaves one. There has to be a third person, someone dedicated to ridding whichever one of us is left to make that call tomorrow."

He squinted, digesting her remark. Then he pointed the fork at her and shook it with the sausage attached. "You're onto something that makes a lot of sense. There's no way they're going to let either of us walk away from this, simply because we know too much already. We know to what extent they'll go to get what they want."

"I think we should get out of here now. We're sitting ducks if we stay," she mentioned hastily.

"Let's not be too quick. Getting out of here now would just complicate matters. We wouldn't be prepared for anything they might decide to throw at us. Plus we'd not be as strong if we were separated. Staying would at least give us an opportunity to defend ourselves together. We've got to come up with a plan of our own," he said.

"We don't even know who might be after us. Or when they'll show up," she noted.

Casper shrugged. "I don't know, but I'm sure it'll be before one of us is supposed to walk out of here. I bet they worked out how to get rid of us before we were asked to join."

"I don't like this," she admitted, glancing uneasily across the living room behind her shoulder. "I feel like someone could break in at any moment and we'd not be prepared."

"Nobody is going to break in. Relax. I'll double check that all the doors are locked before we turn in for the night. You've got nothing to worry about. You're safe," he assured.

"Safe until they decide to bust out a window," she blurted.

He sighed and stretched upright, rearing his shoulders for a moment while leaning his head to one side and then the other before slouching forward and relaxing again. "Now you're overthinking too much. They're not going to break through a window. I'd hear them if they tried."

"Overthinking?! That's really what you think?!" she snapped back quickly.

"I'll stay awake all night and sit outside your bedroom if I have to. Just let me handle it," he replied.

Apparently, she had nothing more to say. Her stunned mind was having difficulty maneuvering around everything he just now said, because it was the sweetest comment that a man had ever made to her.

Finally, Casper stuffed the sausage in his mouth after holding it baited on the fork for what seemed like forever. He studied her and grinned while chewing it down enough to swallow. Perhaps he got a kick out of making remarks which left her speechless. Whatever pleasure he took from silencing her, quickly escalated the smirk into a smile.

"I'd hate for all your memories of our time together to be plagued with anxiety and depression," he said.

"Yeah. Well they've really had a rough start," she nearly whispered.

He analyzed her for a moment, as if debating how she might react to what he'd say next. "I guess we possibly could find something to entertain ourselves that would change how you look back on all this."

He suspected that her response could go either way, but she didn't give him anything he thought was possible.

She didn't smile.

Didn't seem surprised.

She only locked eyes with him and raised one brow in probable curiosity.

145

CHAPTER FIFTEEN

"All rise!" called out the bailiff, standing alongside a door at the front left end of the courtroom across from the witness stand and judge's bench.

Liam turned from his podium to find just a handful of people in attendance. There were nine exactly; an amount much less than the number he spent processing through the legal system a few days ago. He looked at them individually but didn't stare. From the halfway decent thirty-something year old brunette that attempted to present herself nicely by wearing a wrinkled white sundress, to the bearded bald man in jeans and T-shirt with his arms sleeved with tattoos - they all reflected the same impression to him; lower class degenerates of society. Believing himself superior to the general population, Liam straightened the tie on the shirt underneath his gray suit jacket and turned his back on the individuals that were his responsibility to prosecute.

The door opened and Alfonso entered the room, wearing the dreaded black gown. He crossed behind the witness stand and trekked up the steps to his bench, without acknowledging the attorneys or individuals scheduled to appear before him. Wheeling his chair backwards to make room for himself, he sat down and the first thing he did was put on a pair of gold frame bifocals.

"Be seated!" he spoke gruffly, finally looking ahead and doing a quick silent count of everyone who showed for judgment.

The court clerk sitting in a small station of her own on the opposite side of the judge's bench reached up and placed a stack of folders on the table in front of him. Alfonso didn't thank her. In fact, he didn't give her any attention. Instead, he pulled the top folder from the stack and laid it open to start their proceedings.

"Darla Martin!" he called out to the room.

The woman in the sundress quietly stood and made her way through the swing door to approach the podium across from Liam. One of the five attorneys huddled all together, gradually separated from the group and joined Darla in her appearance. He placed the only file he had with him on the podium and opened it.

Liam stepped over in front of a table beside him and fumbled through his own stack of folders until finding one labeled *Darla Martin* and withdrawing it from the pile. He returned behind the podium, opening the folder.

"What do we have here, Liam, is this a petit larceny second offense charge?" Alfonso asked, checking his paperwork.

"Yes, your Honor, it is," Liam replied.

Alfonso glanced at the defense attorney. "Jonathan, does your client understand and agree to the charge that brings her before me today?"

"Your Honor, my client wasn't aware that the items she took into her possession were stolen property. They were given to her by a friend to sell online. She had no prior knowledge about where they came from," Jonathan addressed.

"It is an unfortunate situation but having knowledge or none at all does not alter the fact that a crime was committed. Had she not accepted whatever items in the first place, then she would not have risked getting herself in this predicament," Alfonso explained.

"I understand, your Honor, but my client-"

"I would like to point out that Miss Martin's first conviction also involved posting stolen items for sale online. In that case, she addressed to the court that such items were given to her by a friend," Liam interrupted.

"Point noted," Alfonso replied, scanning the paper beneath him. Then he looked at Jonathan and the defendant. "Miss Martin, are you aware this charge, if convicted, carries a maximum penalty of twelve months in jail and a fine of up to twenty-five hundred dollars, with a minimum mandatory incarceration of thirty days?"

"Yes, sir," she whispered nervously.

"All right. Jonathan, I am going to find your client guilty of the larceny charge. I'm hereby sentencing her to the minimum thirty days and setting a fine at no more than one thousand two hundred and fifty dollars. Are you okay with this, Liam?" Alfonso asked, addressing both men at once.

"Yes, your Honor, I'm satisfied with that," Liam answered.

"Your Honor, my client would like to request that she serve her time during weekends," Jonathan mentioned.

Alfonso observed her for a moment. "Miss Martin, are you employed?"

"Umm, yes, sir. I work part time, and I've got two

children," she confirmed, with her voice stressfully trembling. "One is eleven and the other's four. My oldest is autistic and so I don't really have anyone that can take care of him the way I do."

He picked up a pen and took note of her statement. "Okay. I'll approve for you to report on weekends, starting two weekends after the upcoming. Is that fine with you?"

"Yes, sir," she said.

"I hope you've learned a valuable lesson here today, Miss Martin. If I see you in my courtroom again, for any reason, then I'll not be so lenient. You have two children that need a mother in their lives. Straighten up. You're dismissed," he remarked, closing the file and handing it down to the clerk.

A teary eyed Darla Martin bowed her head and pulled away from the podium. Jonathan, her defense attorney, followed closely behind.

Alfonso removed the next folder from the stack and flipped it open. "Bryce Lynwood!" he announced.

Another attorney stepped up to the podium.

No one present for their appearance stood in acknowledgement of the name.

"Bryce Lynwood!" Alfonso repeated, browsing over the attendees.

Still, nobody came forward.

A displeasing disposition suddenly overcame him because a failure to appear was blatant disrespect. He glanced at Liam, shaking his head.

Then he turned and shot a fierce glance at the defense attorney. "Have you spoken with your client recently about his court date?"

"I tried reaching him twice this week, your Honor. I left a voicemail, both times, but Mister Lynwood failed to get back in touch with me," the attorney shared.

"I would like to add that this is the second time Mister Lynwood has missed his court date," Liam communicated.

"I'm going to issue a capias for FTA, and tack on an additional charge to the ones pending," Alfonso mentioned, jotting notes on his paperwork before closing the file and giving it to the clerk.

He retrieved the next folder and glimpsed ahead to see the defense attorney still hadn't removed himself from the podium. "We're finished. Thank you," he stated.

The visibly disappointed attorney nodded and stepped away from the podium.

"Dominique Crenshaw!" Alfonso called for the next defendant.

The bearded man with tattoo covered arms stood from the bench and came strutting through the swing door. He was joined at the podium by his attorney. Dominique smirked while giving the judge his undivided attention; evidently he was unbothered that his fate was in the hands of the justice system.

Alfonso recognized the discourteous gesture but refrained from saying anything because it would only incite the client's rude behavior.

"Mister Crenshaw stands before us with two charges, your Honor. He was arrested on June seventeenth for illegal possession of a controlled substance and assault on a family member," Liam spoke up.

Alfonso eyed the attorney alongside Dominique. "Is

your client aware of the legal consequences accompanying the charges against him?"

"Yes, your Honor," the attorney answered.

Alfonso adjusted his bifocals. "And how does the defendant plead?"

The attorney smiled cockily. "Actually, your Honor, I had a conversation with Mister Rivera before today and we reached an agreement."

"Oh. Is this correct?" Alfonso asked, quickly fixing his gaze on Liam.

"Yes. This is correct, your Honor. Each charge is a first offense, so I'd like to request that Mister Crenshaw's case be placed under advisement," Liam clarified.

"Mister Rivera, would you please approach the bench?" Alfonso asked.

Liam stepped out from behind the podium and confidently neared the bench. He arrived at the side away from the clerk's station to prevent her from overhearing any sensitive information that might get leaked during their discussion.

"What's the meaning of all this?" Alfonso whispered, after leaning forward and far enough to the side for the clerk not to hear. "Why the hell have you gone behind my back and agreed to overlook such serious charges?"

"Calm down, Alfonso. They're first offense charges. It isn't like you're going to throw the book at him for either one," Liam stated.

"That's not the point. The point is you went behind my back and cut your little deal without giving me a reason first. Now I am going to look like the asshole if I disagree,"

Alfonso hissed.

Liam knocked once on top of the wood frame in front of him. "You are not going to disagree. We might be able to use this guy at some point down the road."

"I thought you said you were done recruiting guys after the last two you conned into our scheme? Also, I told you that I'm not getting myself involved with any more of your dealings once this one is finished," Alfonso argued.

Liam smiled. "I'm not dragging you into anything else. Your grumpy ass is going to retire like planned. I'm not signing him on to do anything, either. I just think it would be a good idea to have him as backup, in case we ever need him for something."

"Like what?" Alfonso inquired.

"I don't know," Liam breathed. "But if I continue to stand here and go back and forth with you about it, then we're likely to draw attention to ourselves. So be a good sport, and stick with taking the case under advisement."

Liam took a step back before Alfonso could get in another word. He turned and surveyed Dominique, winking at him to communicate that all was well while on his way back to the podium.

"All right, Mister Crenshaw. The choice I'm making isn't how I ordinarily handle affairs but I'm going to agree with Mister Rivera and take your case under advisement. If you abstain from conflict with law enforcement for the next sixty days, then I will consider lessening, with a possibility of dismissing, the charges brought against you."

Dominique bowed his head, smiling, while his attorney patted him on the back. "Thank you, your Honor."

"Mister Rivera, is there anything you would like to add?" Alfonso asked.

Liam turned to Dominique's attorney. "I would like to make known that if Mister Crenshaw fails to abide by the orders of the court, then I will strive to convict and push to have him sentenced with the maximum punishment applicable for each offense."

Alfonso monitored Liam with disgust. What repulsed him the most was how Liam's arrogance portrayed itself above the law. Something else bothersome was the way he flirted with bolstering his own illegal involvements in front of a blind society. He flaunted too much power, and Alfonso wasn't exactly sure when in the past his colleague acquired this authoritarian influence.

Liam's demeanor provided the impression that he believed himself to be the supreme force.

Judge.

Jury.

Executioner.

CHAPTER SIXTEEN

Elliot rolled onto his side upon the grungy bed in a cluttered room that was darkened by a blanket nailed to the wall and concealing the window. The only light spilling into the room came from the dim hallway outside the bedroom doorway which Darlene left wide open after whatever time she sneaked out of bed without waking him.

He coughed and groaned, not wanting to get up. His head was grinding and throbbing inside with a hangover resulting from overindulging one too many oversized bottles of beer last night. It was the type of headache that punched his temples from within when he barely moved. He slid across the mattress, despite suffering what felt like two screwdrivers twisting behind his eyes. Normally, he didn't give much thought to his side of the bed being butted against the wall but during this inconvenient moment, he regretted the fact since it hurt to move.

He touched his feet on the floor and sat there for a moment, surrendering to his ailments. Aside from the headache, he was coping with an erection stretching inside his draggled piss stained underwear. Darlene may have been the early bird but she obviously didn't get the worm. Her failure to satisfy him before abandoning did irk him a bit, because her grimy hot pocket was a suitable enough cum dumpster to begin his day on a positive note.

154

After sitting on the bed for a while longer, he comprehended a vague but skunky odor around him. He hadn't recognized this stale fragrance prior to this morning. Thinking that he might know the origin, Elliot slid one hand inside the crusty underwear and rubbed the stiff length of his clammy penis. Then he withdrew and raised his hand beneath his nose. One quick sniff and he jerked his hand away, snarling his face. The odor on his fingers was strongly repulsive. Darlene may have showered last night but the soap bar didn't disguise the natural indelicacy burrowed deep in her crotch. Now that the moisture from her inside had dried and stayed on his dick all night, it smelled like something fermenting.

"Nasty ass bitch," he huffed.

He spit and his saliva splattered across a plastic bag laying on the floor. He stood and partly staggered around the front of the bed, dodging a variety of obstacles strung upon the floor.

"Darlene?!" he yelled, stepping into the hallway. "Are you here, or did you take your filthy ass back to the house?!"

Silence pursued his voice.

"Better have taken your ass home," he mumbled, turning right and walking through the doorway to the only room between his bedroom and the living room. "After leaving your goddamn funk of puss rot on me."

Elliot flipped the lightswitch while making an immediate left turn. He looked in the mirror and saw his reflection soiled by scattered specs of dry toothpaste and cloudy patches of residue buildup on the glass. He gave the room a quick look over; the shower curtain was pulled open with the sud caked bar of soap laying inside the tub, and both lids on the toilet were raised which provided him with a view of the yellow pond in the bowl. Evidently Darlene made herself at home and didn't tidy up afterward, because he was positive that he wasn't the last person to urinate and shower.

Elliot concentrated on the mirror again, shaking his head. Darlene certainly knew every trick to piss him off, however, he was adamant about not letting her reprehensible actions get under his skin at the moment. Right now, he was focused on preparing his mind for the task ahead. Hired hitman was never in his job description. He was used to peddling narcotics, forging checks, and disturbing the peace; taking someone's life was an entirely different ballgame. This was not something he thought he couldn't do; truthfully, he knew it was in him to get the job done, and with the right preparation he'd not feel sympathetic toward his victims - which was his greatest concern. After the fact, of course.

He turned his head slightly while studying his reflection and touched the side of his face. Stubbles of hair weren't visible but his jaw felt like he was gliding his fingers along sandpaper. Turning forward again, he reached down and picked up a can of foam shaving cream. His face wasn't in desperate need of razor treatment but - at his age - if the babyface helped generate a youthful appearance, then he'd vigorously stick to performing high-end maintenance.

He gave the can two hard shakes before dispensing a mound of aqua blue cream on his hand. Then he returned the can on the back of the sink and put his hands together, spreading the paste into a thick lather. He smeared the foam on his jaws, around his mouth, and across the suprahyoid triangle under his chin. Afterwards he turned the cold water on, rinsed excess foam off his hands, and then turned the handle again until a small stream flowed. The last thing he did prior to analyzing himself was grab the five-blade razor that was also on the back of the sink.

Observing himself, Elliot collected a sense of unfamiliarity. He had drastically changed from an individual he barely remembered to the profligate he was today, and he plummeted into the abyss of a downward spiral so quickly that he could vaguely recall where it all began. Unfortunately, the depth of pain inside those menacing eyes staring back at him was there to remind when and how it started. He wanted to pull away from reminiscing but was compelled to recollect the harrowing tragedy he struggled for years to steer away from remembrance.

"Emma," he whispered, plunging into the midst of hurt in eyes that did not blink.

All that it had taken was him pronouncing a long lost name and everything came rushing back.

The scenic landscape.

His surroundings.

What he rediscovered felt like an occurrence that happened yesterday.

The front of the car faced the river, and about ten feet away from either side was a dense thicket of woodland, gated by thorn bushes. Beyond the trunk were two narrow dirt tracks where grass had been scalped by countless motorists frequenting this popularized private hangout.

Undoubtedly, this trail led back to a main road somewhere not visible from the location.

The view beyond the windshield offered the width of the river. On the opposite side stood a staggering height of cliffs topped with more woodland, and it all stretched as far across as the eye could see. There were no boats on the water. Not one person in sight.

Sex And Candy by Marcy Playground was halfway through playing on the portable CD player plugged into the vehicle's lighter port. The volume wasn't cranked too loud. Perhaps it should have been, though, because feminine gasps and groans sounded a pitch away from drowning out the song's vocals.

The driver and passenger were in an awkward position, with the male driver leaning on top of the female passenger from across the center console while she sat twisted toward him halfway. Her hair was out of sorts and tangled from him brushing through and pulling it aggressively. His other arm was elbow deep inside the bottom of her shirt as he groped and squeezed one breast inside its bra cup. The young lady leaned her head back and looked at the roof of the car while his lips bathed in the warmth of her neck. Suddenly she winced, wiggled, and pushed his shoulders, as if she was uncomfortable with how she was positioned.

She sniffed forcibly, and pressed harder against his shoulders. "Stop. We can't do this right now. What if somebody comes down here?"

He broke from her neck long enough to say, "Ain't nobody gonna come down here. This is our spot for now."

"People come here all the time," she mentioned.

He disregarded her statement and intensified his drive by switching from kissing her neck to sticking out his tongue and licking it. Slowly, he slid up her neck, drooling as he maneuvered his way up to her ear. He curved his tongue and brushed the tip against the bottom hindside of her ear before leaning upward and grasping its entire bottom half with his teeth. He applied just enough pressure to make her groan, and pulled gently.

She squirmed and nudged him again - this time following a doublefisted strike on his chest. "Elliot, I'm serious, not here!"

Annoyed by her, he jerked away and slumped in the driver's seat with his back against the door. The dissatisfied glow in the eyes of a young twenty-something Elliot Thomspson created an uncomfortable situation where not even he knew what to expect.

He pressed his thumb on the side of his nose and sealed one nostril while snorting through the other, inhaling whatever had it clogged.

"Shit was supposed to mellow you out. So why are you sitting over there, stressing?" he asked.

"I just don't want anybody that might know my father to see me. I don't need anyone running back and telling him what I do. He's hard on me without knowing what I do. If he knew everything I did, then I'd never be allowed out of the house," she indicated.

"No one's gonna get close enough to see what we're doing. I mean hell, Emma, we can plainly see if anyone was to show up before they even get close," he alleged.

Her lips twisted with uncertainty. "That is not the point. Everyone knows what goes on down here, and I'm not okay with it."

He reached over and took her left hand. The same hand which displayed the two-stone engagement ring that she excitedly accepted when he proposed three months ago. He swiped his thumb across the stones and up against her knuckle.

"Who cares what other people think? We're getting married. What we do is our business," he stated.

"I care!" Emma chirped, yanking her hand out from under him and scooting back against the door. "Just because we're getting married doesn't mean we can do whatever the hell we want. My dad doesn't like that we're engaged, so it wouldn't take a whole lot to set him off. All he's got to do is catch wind that I did something he doesn't approve of and my ass would get grounded for life."

He huffed in frustration. "Are you positive you sniffed the Xanax? You ain't acting like you did."

She sneered directly. "Yes, I did! You were sitting right there and watched me."

"Your ass should be calm as fuck right now but it ain't. Instead, you're tripping balls over something that ain't all that important," he reacted.

"Maybe it's best if you just take me home," she brazenly stated.

He chuckled. "Nah. I ain't giving your daddy that much power over us. He ain't controlling anything we do."

He reached in front of her seat and opened the glove box, slipping his hand inside and pulling out a white square prescription bottle.

"I'm not doing another Xanax," she assured him.

He slammed the door on the glove box and leaned

back on the driver's seat with the bottle in hand. "I'm not giving you one. It's something better."

"Like what?" she inquired timorously.

He unscrewed the lid and dumped a single green pill on his hand. Quickly, he fastened the cap and tucked the bottle between his legs.

"You'll see," he replied, cramming his hand inside the thin space between the driver's seat and middle console, and withdrawing a CD case that had its interior cover pamphlet removed.

"I am not taking something that I don't know what it is," she stressed.

He raised the case with the clear side toward him and noticed a cloudy yellow residue on the plastic. Apparently he knew the source of the debris because he brought the case closer to him and ran his tongue across it. Then he lowered it with the clear side on his leg and brushed the case against his jeans, attempting to dry the plastic by giving it a few hard scrubs. Afterwards, he turned it over and left it lying on his leg while reaching inside his left pants pocket and retrieving a crumpled dollar bill.

"It's just an Oxy-eighty. It ain't gonna kill you," he said, placing the pill over the president's face and folding all sides of the bill on top of it.

"I'm not doing that. You wanted me to do the Xanax and I did," she vented.

"You better come down off your high horse. I'm giving this to you and you're gonna do it. Now stop acting like your daddy," he advised.

A hostile expression abruptly overcame her, with a trace amount of disbelief, but she didn't say anything in defense of his statement. Actually, she didn't speak at all. Perhaps she learned not to react soundly after several failed altercations with him in the past. Elliot was unapologetically cruel in the verbal sense; maybe she didn't want to instigate and discover how malignant he could become in other ways.

He put the folded money between his teeth and bit down. After feeling the pill break and crumble, he spun the bill around and bit again.

"This'll just knock the edge off. The Xanax should have, but, well, obviously you've got a tolerance for 'em," he said, lowering the bill and unraveling it above the case.

She watched him pour pieces of broken pill onto the case. When no more particles fell out of the money, he folded it in half and rubbed the sides together. Then he snatched the prescription bottle between his legs and pressed its lid down against the CD case, crushing pill crumbs that didn't get completely broken when he attempted biting the pill into fine powder.

"This is absurd. I can't believe I'm about to do this," she expressed, avoiding saying what she truly thought in order to prevent stimulating a negative reaction.

"It's all good. Nothing's gonna bother you after this. You'll be totally kicked back and relaxed," he mentioned, stretching one long powder line by forming it with a plastic gas station rewards card that he picked up from one of two cup holders between their seats.

Uncertain about how she should respond, especially since she didn't agree, Emma remained quiet.

He took a short piece of plastic straw from the same cup holder that housed the rewards card and reached it and the CD case in front of her. She looked at him for a moment, confused.

"Are you not going to do some?" she asked.

He laughed briefly. "Nah. I've done enough shit today. I don't need anything else."

"So you want me to do all of this?" she inquired.

"If I didn't want you to do it, then don't you think I wouldn't have crushed the whole damn thing?" he asked.

"How messed up is this going to get me?" she questioned, taking the straw. "I don't want to confront my dad later and still be feeling whatever effects, because he'll know I'm on something."

He shrugged. "I mean at the most you'll be relaxed. Like nothing is gonna bother you. You're not gonna trip balls and say dumb shit, if that's what you're worried about."

Emma pushed her hair behind her ears to stop it from hanging below her face and potentially causing a mess when she leaned over the case. She put the straw to her nostril and began sniffing.

Suddenly she jerked away, pressing the palm of her hand against her eye. "Okay! I don't know if I can do the rest. My fucking nose is on fire."

"Oh, come on, pansy," he uttered.

She sniffled until feeling her nasal cavity clear, and went back to leaning over the case with the straw in her nose. She inhaled the rest of the powderized pill and pulled away, coughing a few times.

"Oh my god! I can't believe I just did that!" she shrieked, setting the straw on the case and then covering her nose as an intense burn wrapped her brain.

"Good girl. Now that wasn't so bad, was it?" he asked, tossing the straw in the cup holder before sliding the CD case into the slim space between the middle console and his seat.

She batted her teary eyes. "It wouldn't be if the burning stopped."

After some time passed with them continuing basic conversation, Elliot picked up the CD player and skipped from one song to the next. On to the next. He forwarded through songs until hearing the start of *Mr. Jones* by Counting Crows. He set the player down and allowed the song to go on undisturbed.

"I think I'm really starting to feel it," Emma mentioned.

"Oh yeah, how are you feeling?" he asked.

She grinned, and almost giggled. Her eyes appeared less lively, as if taken by superior comfort. "I don't know. It's hard to describe. I'm way too calm. There are no constant thoughts racing through my head."

Reaching out and touching the back of her face, he slipped his fingers on the back of her neck and leaned her toward him.

"How's this feel?" he whispered, before touching her lips with his mouth and grazing her teeth with the end of his tongue.

"That feels so good," she said softly, without trying to push him away this time.

Taking her words as a representation of approval, he leaned her back against the door and eased himself on top of her before kissing her lower lip and then making his way beneath the side of her face. He laid his hand on the top of the inner side of her leg and slowly worked his way inside the bottom of her windbreaker shorts. Progressing onward, he landed on the warm pit of her inner thigh and massaged there while drifting his tongue against her neck.

"Elliot, I don't know if-"

Strangely, her tame voice ceased.

He panted in her ear and intensified every way he handled her within the scope of arousal. His teeth tested the sensitivity in her neck by pinching various areas. The hand nestled crotch deep inside her shorts began grinding the depth of her inner thigh. His thumb stretched across her panties, delivering repetitive austere treatment.

"You don't know what?" he asked.

"I don't know," she whispered.

As he kissed and fondled her more intensely, Emma suddenly responded in a way opposite of how he expected. She sank - entirely relaxed - in the seat beneath him. Her hand that draped across the back of his neck fell on her chest between them, and her head turned away from him - expanding the length of neck that he dedicated the majority of his time focusing on.

He slid up and bit the bottom of her ear much harder than any time prior, hoping to get a response.

Emma didn't make a sound.

He couldn't get her to stop moving earlier, however, now she just laid there.

Thinking that he might not be doing enough to rouse excitement, he smashed his thumb against her panties and scrubbed diligently.

"You like that, baby?" he gasped.

Surprisingly, she didn't answer.

He couldn't even get a grunt out of her during all of the effort he put into trying to gratify her.

Her behavior in the situation didn't seem right. He withdrew his hand from her shorts and pulled back from laying on top of her. Reaching on the side of her face pressed against the seat, he turned her head forward to get a clear view. At some point during the process of straightening her head, hair came loose behind one ear and smeared across her eyes and nose. He brushed those sweaty strands to the side of her head and recognized that her eyes were closed.

"Emma!" he called out, grabbing under her chin and shaking her head.

Her eyes stayed shut. She didn't react to the physical contact and she did not respond to him screaming in her face.

He smacked her cheek lightly. "Baby, wake up!"

She did no such thing.

He looked down and around at everything surrounding him but had no idea what he was looking for, if anything really. Things happened quickly which didn't provide him enough time to think about what he should do next. He looked at her again, grabbing her shoulders and shaking them aggressively.

"Dammit, Emma, wake up!" he yelled.

No amount of screaming at or jarring her concluded with positive results. There was not anything semi about it, she was unconscious.

He glanced at his surroundings once more. Still, not one thought about what to do came to mind, and not knowing how to respond frustrated him. Then he caught a glimpse of the rear view mirror and something in his mind clicked. Without giving it much thought, he reached up and grabbed the mirror, pulling and twisting until he broke it away from the windshield. Giving the mirror side a quick swipe against his shirt, he reached over and held it under her nose with the glass facing her. Perhaps he believed that he would see moisture cloud the glass from her breathing out of her nose. Unfortunately, he didn't see any change in the clarity of the mirror.

"Goddammit!" he roared, slinging the mirror to the backseat.

He pulled away from Emma, placed his elbows on the wheel, and laid his head in both hands. All that he could do was think about her father's reaction and nothing to do with her well-being. Thinking past her father kicking his ass, he considered the legal consequences. He technically murdered her, although accidentally. The law wouldn't give him a slap on the wrist over an unintentional mishap, though; actually, he'd likely be looking at facing a minimum of twenty-five years. Maybe longer, since he was also in possession of controlled substances.

He grabbed her shirt collar and twisted it around his hand once before jerking her forward, almost out of the seat. He jounced her one last time in another failed effort to revive consciousness. Disgracing all fondness for his fiancee, he let her go and she crashed backwards against the passenger door, slamming the back of her head on the window.

Getting off the river was the only thought racing through his mind, but he had enough wits to know that he couldn't go into town with her slouched in the seat. Not wanting to waste any more time and risk seeing the arrival of another horny couple, he reached across and opened the door behind her. Emma exited the vehicle halfway which allowed her head to touch the ground. Then he opened his door and hopped out of the seat to fast-track around the front of the vehicle.

Quickly, he crouched and reached underneath her arms, dragging her into tall grass a few feet away from where he parked. He suspected nobody would find her this far off the trail because what people mostly did here was sit in their automobile and fulfill their desire to swap bodily fluids.

Giving what he considered was a proper send-off by crossing her hands on her abdomen, Elliot got down on one knee and slowly swept hair away from her face before bending further and kissing her droughty lips. Then he stood and the shelter of wild grass quickly overlaid her presence. Able to see just a fraction of her face, he stared with the intent to immortalize her beauty in the curse of memory.

The horrible expression that befell him on that day was the same wretched face looking back at him from the mirror. He was damn certain that no one would find her in the untreated landscape, but somebody did discover Emma shortly before night settled. Luckily, he was never linked to or charged in relation to her death, although he did get heavily interrogated by the authorities and her father. Emma's mother was too distraught to involve herself in the matter.

Unfortunately, what he learned much later, after the

autopsy results came back, was that Emma's official time of death was seven minutes past the time he laid her in the grass. This revelation sickened him because he felt that there was something he could have done to save her; dropped her off a block away from the hospital and allowed a random passerby to get the proper medical assistance. Abandonment resulting in what should have been an avoided tragedy was sure to haunt him for the duration of his life. It had changed him already - creating a despicably remorseless monster of a once emotionally connected man.

Numb to the razor slicing his cheek, Elliot witnessed blood seep beyond the foam layer of shaving cream but was too absorbed by misery to let it concern him.

Instead of cleansing the area like an ordinary person would do, he allowed his blood to stream before it curved and flowed to the bottom center of his chin, where constant beads dropped and splattered in the sink below.

CHAPTER SEVENTEEN

The evening was blissful compared to the alternate reality that everyone involved had intended.

Shei held what she believed was her fifth glass of wine for the evening. Truthfully, it might be her sixth; she lost count after three and only assumed that what she thought was true. Regardless of how many glasses she consumed, it didn't matter because she had achieved alcohol induced carelessness. There was no stress about devising an exit strategy, although coming up with a plan to get out of this mess should be a priority. She endured much chaos since the start of things, and the opportunity to pull back and comfortably enjoy herself felt reasonable.

She took a sip from the glass and quickly licked beneath her lip, catching a lone driblet that somehow avoided consumption. Then she set the glass on the island and spun herself halfway to one side without raising off the stool.

She gazed at Casper, smiling. "I remember you said that you've not had any real luck with the ladies, but do you have kids?"

He shook his head when replying, "No kids."

She crossed her arms on the island and leaned forward, staggering all of her weight to one side. Quietly, she watched him, gathering the impression that alcohol hadn't impaired him as much as it did her. He was stable on his feet, not swaying, and seemed attentively aware of everything going on around him. She didn't know how much he drank up to now but he was obviously capable of tolerating more than what was in her ability. Perceiving her vision slightly skewed, Shei trusted that if she stood off the stool then she'd probably smack the floor flat on her ass.

"Do you want any?" she asked.

His brows lifted as he examined her with uncertainty. "Kids?" he inquired.

She giggled. "Yes, silly. What did you think I was talking about?"

He shrugged, playfully smirking at the same time. "When it comes to you, I'm not sure. Especially right now."

She squinted her eyes at him. "What is that supposed to mean?"

"Look at you. One wrong move and you're going to go to the floor," he said, laughing.

"Hey! I'm not drunk," she declared.

He stood away from leaning against the counter next to the sink and approached the stool across from her. "You're not exactly sober either."

"I'm decent," she avowed, sitting up straight in a way to demonstrate herself as being better off than what she actually was.

Casper set his glass on the island and took a seat in front of her. He saw the gloss in her eyes wasn't bloodshot but it was close to becoming.

"Well…" she voiced, leering at him like he was supposed to have said something already.

"Umm, what?" he asked.

"Do you want kids?" she inquired, steadily holding him in her gaze.

He took a long, deep breath and then huffed. "I did a few years ago but there's no way I could handle the commotion nowadays. The older I get, the less patience I've got. I doubt that I'd be able to tolerate the all night crying and constant bottle feeding."

"It's not that bad," she stated, grabbing her glass by the rim, picking it up, and giving the wine a swirl. "My daughter was pretty manageable during infancy. She really didn't cry much throughout the night. And I breastfed her, so there was no hassle in having to constantly prepare formulas."

He chuckled and pressed both hands on his chest. "I'm obviously not equipped, therefore, heating bottles to the right temperature would be my burden."

She smiled and lowered her head, looking at the bare stretch of island in front of her. "I think you'd make a decent father."

"Yeah? I think you've had too much to drink," he joked.

Elliot stopped the vehicle in the middle of the road and shut off the ignition when the two-story cabin became visible in the distance.

He turned off the lights.

Although night was only an hour or so away from falling, his financial freedom remained perceptible on the horizon.

Several things wasted little time crossing his mind.

He recollected draping the plastic bag over Shei's head and the empowerment he felt during that moment overwhelmed him all over again. Hearing little Sierra's child voice ask if he was a superhero resurfaced to haunt him. Lastly, his remembrance of reminding Darlene what she was going to do without choice played out. Each memory pertained to the lives of other people and he felt no sympathy for them.

He exited the vehicle and cautiously shut the door. Of course, Shei and Casper couldn't hear whatever sounds he might potentially make, but he didn't want to risk making the improbable a possibility.

He opened the rear driver's side door and fetched the McMillan TAC 50 sniper rifle from the seat. He'd been carrying this weapon ever since he agreed to the job, waiting to test its precision. Without closing the door, he pulled the strap over his shoulder and strode toward the woodland.

His destination - three enormous rocks wedged together and standing tall - stood in the woods about forty yards away from the road. The center one was the tallest and flat on top. He scaled the first rock with ease and experienced minor difficulty climbing onto the second. His only challenge had been to acquire a grip good enough to support him dragging his weight up the side.

Once on the surface, he shed the strap and brought the rifle ahead of him before laying on his side. He pointed the barrel forward and looked through the scope, slightly repositioning his aim until getting a clear view beyond the trees and through the large left window displaying a broad area of the living room and kitchen. The center of his scope honed in on the back of Shei's head.

His finger curled around the trigger.

He breathed in and held, knowing he'd have to be fast and unflinching if he was going to get off two successful shots.

Seconds after Casper made some offhand remark, Shei forgot what he said but must have thought it was humorous because she burst out laughing. She cackled so hard that she leaned too far to one side and fell off the stool, striking the floor on her side instead of crashing ass first.

A mild crackling sound ricocheted throughout the kitchen from the living room.

"Fucking hell!" Casper howled painfully.

Shei heard a loud thump on the backside of the island and immediately assumed that he, too, had plummeted to the floor. She glimpsed across the narrow width of kitchen space but could not see him because he was literally behind the island.

"Stay on the ground!" he squalled, unsure about what she was doing since he couldn't see her either.

"What happened?" she asked, lowering her stomach on the floor and trembling as she scooted across the tile to try making her way to him.

"Stay where you are!" he advised.

She froze. "What's going on?!"

He looked down at his hand pressed against the front of his shoulder and saw blood oozing between his fingers before trickling down the back of his hand. He withdrew from holding his shoulder and all that he could see was a small rip in the fabric surrounded by significant blood loss continuing to stain through his shirt. Beneath the fabric, severe pain scorched deep inside his flesh, almost touching the bone. He pressed the wound again, assuming that it was the only way to minimize bleeding, and slid toward the bottom level cabinets behind him.

"I'm shot," he stated.

"What?!" she shrieked.

He slammed back against one of the cabinet doors. "Whoever is hired to take us out is here. They got me pretty good but it's tolerable. I'll live."

"Oh my god!" she squealed, placing her hands over her head. "This is it. We're going to die."

"We're not going to die," he pledged, scooting to the side of the kitchen away from her. Maybe he didn't want her seeing him in this condition because she would totally freak out and draw the attention of the individual who had come to hunt them.

"I've got an idea. I want you to lay still while I make a break to get out of sight. Pretend that you're dead. They might not know that you weren't hit," he added.

"That's a terrible idea," she complained, keeping both hands on her head when turning and glancing into the living room. "It's obvious that I've not been hit, so how is that going to do me any good?"

He winced as pain spread throughout his shoulder. "Dammit, you're right. Okay. I want you to come around to this side and stay hidden. I'll take a different position and wait for them to come check the place. The only way we're going to get out of here is by fighting back."

"All right," she whispered, laying her hands on the tile and crawling forward. "I'm coming around."

She maneuvered around the backside of the island and to her surprise, Casper was nowhere to be seen. He left behind traces of his injury smeared on the floor but not enough for her to consider that he was in grave danger. There were just a few bloody handprints dragged upon the floor and none of them indicated where he might have gone.

"Hey," she called out quietly, crawling toward the center of the island. "Where'd you go?"

Silence trailed her voice.

"Dammit," she griped, realizing that he left her to confront their perpetrator alone.

She scooted next to the stool and thrust her back to the island. The state of being by herself nearly prompted a whirlwind of anxiety. She couldn't wrap her mind around as to why Casper would leave her this way - indefensible and fearing for her life.

Elliot stepped off the rocks and pulled the strap over his shoulder, returning the rifle against his back. Exiting the woods, he bypassed his vehicle and traveled the gravel trail toward the house. He knew that the bullet didn't strike Shei but did see Casper take the hit and get knocked backwards off the stool. He didn't know where the bullet struck him exactly, and so he wasn't positive that the shot killed him.

Shei wasn't anything to worry about. He dealt with her just the other day and learned that she was pathetically weak, even when applying her greatest effort. Really, he didn't put much thought into how he was going to handle her. The only things on his mind were the cash reward and relocation.

After ascending the steps, he tried the door and

found that it was locked. Then he approached the most sensible point of entry, which was the large window with a small hole encircled by long jagged cracks. Clearly, this damage came from his bullet penetrating the glass.

Taking the rifle off his back and aiming the buttstock forward, he rammed ahead and burst through with one strike. Then he plunged one foot forward and kicked out the lower shards that didn't shatter when the rifle struck. Once the space was cleared, he stepped inside the house, and began whistling.

He pointed the barrel at the floor while scanning either side of the living room.

No one came forward.

No one made a sound.

"Y'all might as well show your faces. Ain't no point prolonging the inevitable. Make this easy for me and I'll make it quick for you. Come on out here now. We ain't got all night," he said, crossing between the couch and recliner.

He looked down beside the island, thinking that they couldn't have gone anywhere except behind it. Sure, they could have tried making a run for the upstairs but he didn't believe that was the case because he would've seen their attempt through the scope.

"We can go on and on playing this game, but it's gonna end just as it was meant to," he stated.

Shei bent her legs against her chest and curled her arms around them, trying to compress herself out of plain sight next to the stool. She didn't know who or how many came to exterminate, and she remained clueless about where Casper had gone. As much as she wanted to scream and beg the intruder(s) to show mercy on her, she did what she considered might be best and fought to stay silent.

Elliot made a series of clicking sounds with his tongue smacking the roof of his mouth. "What do we have here? The way we keep having these encounters has got me thinking that something is meant to happen between us. No worries, though. I'll take the liberty to explore more of you after I've buried a bullet in that pretty little head."

"Shit, man. You don't have to do this. Please," she whined, looking up to find that he had stepped past the island and discovered her.

He grinned. "You're right. I don't have to but I'm gonna, for the sake of bettering my life and getting out of this shithole."

"Whatever my father's paying, I'll give you more," she proposed.

He chuckled and shook his head at once. "I'd eagerly take you up on that deal if you were an honest woman, but you can't offer anything close to what your daddy's willing to give. It's a shame, too. A beautiful woman like yourself. I can think up a number of things I'd like to do other than put you six feet in the ground."

"Please... I'll disappear and never speak to anyone. No one has to know what happened, and you'll still get your money. Just don't kill me. I've got a child," she pleaded.

"I apologize in advance, sweetheart, but I am an honest man. If someone hires me to get a job done and they're willing to buy me out with a decent reward, then I'm gonna hold myself true to their request," he said.

Elliot turned and glanced across the short hallway

behind him. The bathroom door was slightly open and all that he could see beyond its slim opening was darkness. Since he couldn't see, he listened but nothing noticeable indicated to him that Casper had fled there. He eyed the door for a few seconds longer, giving all of his attention to the chance of hearing something that might announce Casper's whereabouts. Still, nothing granted him that knowledge.

He turned to Shei again. "Where'd your sidekick go? I know he can't be too far. Where's he? I think I'd rather deal with him first because me and you are gonna have a little fun together."

She covered her face between her knees. "I don't know where he is. Don't you think I'd be with him if I did?"

He raised the barrel at her and slowly curled one finger around the trigger. "If you don't tell me what I wanna hear, then I'm gonna splatter your pretty little brain all over this fucking kitchen. Now my thinking is you don't want me doing that."

"I don't know where he is. I swear," she mumbled.

"Oh. All right. We'll do it your way then." He took a step closer toward her and held the end of the barrel just inches away from the side of her head. "I'll be sure to tell that spoiled kid of yours that mommy went down fighting like a true superhero. I doubt that she'd wanna hear that you sat on your ass, sobbing those eyes out while begging me to spare you. No child wants to hear about how their parents gave up."

He applied pressure on the trigger, however, it wasn't enough to discharge firepower.

"Move!" Casper roared.

Shei slid away from the island without having any knowledge about what was occurring and smacked her back against the refrigerator. When she looked up to process what was going on, she discovered Casper standing behind her would-be attacker and holding a bath towel across his face. The rifle barrel pointed in every direction as Elliot stammered, unable to see his surroundings. Luckily, he never squeezed the trigger.

"Get something!" Casper snapped, gazing at her with angry eyes while struggling to overtake him.

She didn't know what to do. Things were happening too fast for her to consider what either man might do next.

Elliot swung the buttstock behind his side, trying to strike Casper and break his leverage, but Casper moved out of the way in advance and twisted him to face the island. Pushing forward, Casper bent him over the island while maintaining a firm hold of the towel pulled across his face and against the back of his head.

Elliot jerked aggressively and kicked backwards, hitting Casper's legs but failing to gain any distance between them.

Casper shot a disgruntled look over at Shei. "Help me! Do something! I can't hold him down like this forever!"

After scrambling to her feet and swaying on her way to the counter next to the sink, she opened the drawer above the door to one of the bottom cabinets. She couldn't clearly make out anything directly in front of her since panic blurred her sight. A variety of silver, glowing from light in the room shining into the drawer, was all that she could distinguish. Reaching both hands inside the drawer, she fumbled through a mix of forks, spoons, and butter knives. Spoons and forks wouldn't do her any good, of course, and a butter knife would be useless as well. Sinking one hand beneath several layers, she stumbled upon something long, wide, and sharp on one side.

Was it a carving knife?

A cleaver, maybe?

She ran her hand back along the handle before acquiring a grip and jerking the item out of the drawer. The style of knife apparently didn't concern her. Actually, all that mattered was having something sufficient to positively help Casper get the situation under control.

Equipped for confrontation, she turned and rushed toward the men still in a scuffle.

Elliot continued to thresh and kick while his upper body and side of his head pressed the island tabletop. The rifle, wedged between him and the island, was in no position to provide him with the upperhand. Casper held the towel tight across his face and pushed down the loose ends to stop him from jerking his head.

Shei raised the knife but then stalled from doing anything because she wasn't quite sure where to strike.

"Now!" Casper growled.

"Where?!" she shrieked.

"Hell- I don't know! It doesn't matter!" he remarked, leaning forward and planting his forearm across the bottom center of Elliot's back.

She cringed first and then drove the knife down. Elliot let out a painful scream that was muffled by the towel. Casper shook his head, studying the result with disappointment. The tip of the blade barely penetrated the fabric pulled over his head. Blood seeped to the surface and spread around the metal, however, it wasn't enough for either of them to suspect that a life threatening injury had been sustained.

"Come on now. You've got to be more competitive. You barely nicked him. Try again," Casper insisted.

She sighed and raised the knife. Stepping closer to Casper, she nudged him with emphatic bodily contact while acting slightly irritated that she didn't invoke serious harm.

"Well, dammit! If you weren't hogging the area, then I wouldn't be trying to do things from an awkward angle," she griped.

He moved aside, maybe half of a step. "Okay. See if that helps."

She pulled the knife face level, gripping its handle with both hands this time.

It's kill or be killed, she thought.

Evidently, this reminder was all that she needed to get in the appropriate mindset, because she thrust the knife down quickly, sinking half of the blade beneath the towel.

Elliot screamed.

PAHH!

Accidental gunfire obliterated his high pitched voice. Fortunately, the rifle wasn't pointed at anyone and the bullet hit the wall on the outside of the staircase.

Elliot rammed his knees against the front of the island, creating a constant, loud thump. He let out a groan that was nowhere near as loud as his initial scream and attempted raising his chest off the island, but was denied when Casper applied more pressure to pinning him down.

Heavy bleeding saturated the portion of towel surrounding the blade buried just a little more than halfway. Given its placement, Shei appeared to have plunged the knife through his cheek and inside his mouth.

Casper turned his arm forward on Elliot's back before sliding up and gripping his neck. Then he let go of holding the towel, which stayed in place when he pulled away, and grabbed the large wooden knife handle. Quickly, he jerked upwards and cleared the bloodstained blade from being embedded in flesh.

Elliot howled in misery.

Shei placed both hands together over her mouth and nose during the sobering observation of a grisly sight. The sounds of anguish that Elliot produced, accompanied by him pounding the foundation of the island with his knees, and the immeasurable amount of blood absorbing in the towel - all together invented a picture unlike anything she had ever heard or seen.

Without advising her not to watch, Casper swooped down and inserted the knife in what should be the section of skull behind Elliot's eye. He brought his other hand to the handle and propelled every bit of the blade through bone and tough brain matter. Elliot's entire body started twitching violently, causing Shei to wonder if this was how cattle might react after having a captive bolt gun discharged between their eyes. His aggressive jerking lasted for only a long minute, and his agonizing groans lessened until there was no sound.

"Oh shit!" she gasped in shock. "What have we done? We killed him."

Casper let go of the wooden handle, leaving the

knife implanted, and stepped back from leaning against Elliot's lower hindsight. Slowly, Elliot slid backwards until the majority of his weight dragged off the top of the island and sent him colliding with the floor. The towel remained wrapped around his head, concealing the wretched atrocity executed by survival driven hands.

"We've got to call the police. We can't just leave him here and not tell anybody," she said, panicking.

Casper couldn't approach since a dead body stretched across the floor between them but did reach out and grasp her shoulders. "Listen to yourself. You're being ridiculous. We don't have to speak a word, ever. Do you think they're going to report this and mention our involvement? The answer is no, it's very unlikely. This is an ex con in a well respected judge's house. They're not going to want the police, the media hype, or anything else linking this piece of shit back to them. We're good."

She shook her head, gnawed her lip, and wept. "We killed a man."

He jolted her shoulders, believing that it may snap her out of delirium. "That man could have been you. It could have been me. You came into this expecting someone to be killed. We're fortunate that it's neither of us."

She cried silently.

He reached on the side of her face and wiped sideways beneath her eye, smearing wet sorrow along her cheek. "We are fine. It doesn't make sense and it won't for a while, but you're going to call your father tomorrow morning and tell him that the job is done. He'll not know how to react but that should be expected. I'll take care of everything. Trust me. Everything."

CHAPTER EIGHTEEN

Shei sat on her adopted stool, digging one fingernail beneath another on the opposite hand while staring across the room at nothing directly. She was undoubtedly emotionally divided; part of her rejected what they did to Elliot, because all that it accomplished was lowering them on the same level with the vile men that orchestrated this arrangement. But the majority of her mind wholeheartedly accepted what was done - supporting the critical detail Casper said about the matter. The victim easily could have been one of them.

She never dealt with the internally conflicting tug of war the way it severed her mind this evening.

She was present in her surroundings but her mind was completely displaced.

Casper came down off the last step and stood in the walkway between the bathroom and kitchen. He was still wearing the bloodstained shirt but emerged holding a folded white T-shirt and pair of gray mesh shorts at his side. Leaning forward and glimpsing into the kitchen, he saw her sitting at the island and recognized by her facial expression that she was presently imperceptive.

"I'm going to take a quick shower," he stated.

Unsurprisingly, she remained speechless as her eyes stayed fixed in a distant void.

"When I get out, I'll find something to put over the window so that no wildlife drops in for a surprise visit while we're sleeping. Also, you might not want to sit with your back to the window in case our friend there has buddies that we don't know about," he added.

"All that concerns me is getting my daughter back," she said, uninterrupted in her state of tranquility.

"Are you okay?" he inquired, seeing her uniquely unphased.

"Yeah- Yeah, I'm fine. Like you said, they aren't going to jeopardize their intent by getting the police involved. Basically, nothing happened," she replied unpretentiously.

He bowed his head and frowned before turning his back to her. He didn't know what was occurring inside of her head but he didn't like it. The behavior she exhibited filled him with the impression of not knowing what to expect. He didn't enjoy thinking that he would have to keep a watchful eye on her due to concerns about her doing something spontaneously reckless to his safety - or her own.

"I'll be back in a minute. Keep your eyes open and your ears peeled back. If you hear anything, and I mean anything that doesn't sound right, then do not hesitate to inform me," he stated, hoping that assuring her that he'd be quick to return might incapacitate whatever transitory chaos fuming in her head.

She did hear him but was unresponsive. What she didn't hear was the door shut. A moment later, the sound of water jetting out of the overhead shower faucet streamed loud and clear into the kitchen.

Her troubled mind continued to try processing everything that happened. She knew that murder was in the grand scheme of things but wasn't prepared for the way it transpired unexpectedly. For her personally, Elliot was never part of the equation; therefore, his arrival was utterly shocking.

The kill or be killed motto resonated with her since the disturbing realization that she could have been murdered fucked with her head. Everything was all too real now. Nothing was just table talk anymore.

Things about Casper made their way inside her thoughts. How he treated her with gentility and respect was overwhelming in itself. She believed that she handled the extraordinary treatment very well but felt that she could have said or did more to express appreciation. He had no idea what being treated with decency meant to her. To experience a man's capability to show generosity was emotionally refreshing while offering hope that not all men were spineless imbeciles. There was a sense of excitement that she could not condone; nothing tingly, but noticeably energizing.

And then there was the situation with him saving her life. While it may have been unintentional, she realized that she would have taken the bullet if not for being temporarily humored in his presence. Lastly, he rescued her for the second time by intervening when Elliot confronted her one on one.

It all amounted to something truly special when combined. A stranger that knew absolutely nothing about her had not only recovered her from danger but also helped her to feel comfortable being herself.

Her mind wandered into uncharted territory.

From his protective characteristics to the facticity of her finding him attractive. Civil attributes and empathy were a new and exciting experience, but his physical properties seized and retained her attention since the first time she saw him. Every guy she had ever got involved with was handsome in her opinion, but they each lacked the decency in knowing how to treat a woman, which she considered was an important quality. Casper's ability to connect with her on a level she never experienced sparked a curiosity about him. This emotional intrigue caused her to endure an aberrated craving. Her sexual prowess was far-removed from making her a whore, but Casper was the type of man that she'd enjoy getting rough with between the sheets.

Suddenly, her mind backtracked to last night. Thinking about how he held her as they went to sleep all but melted her heart and subdued mental anguish. She desired for so long to be touched like she mattered - with adulation, and solicitude. His treatment of her had gone a long way in disassembling her preconceived perception of him. He was not some inconsiderate monster. Instead, he was the one man that empowered her with the ability to feel feminine for once.

Fear.

Grief.

Excitement.

Inquisitiveness.

This tetrad of emotions steered her into cognitive hysteria. Rational judgment withered beneath the onslaught of potentially disastrous wants. She convinced herself that burdensome past experiences trolled her by cockblocking the life she incontestably deserved, and she was tired of it at the moment.

She no longer wished to be bound by the chains of trauma.

All that she wanted was to be an ordinary woman, free from fear and reaping the rewards of nonpoisonous commitment. She knew the only way to obtain these things was by confronting what frightened her without visualizing the same old nightmarish outcome.

She dragged off the stool and stood away from the island, creeping around the side and tip-toeing to the aperture before the hallway, where she stopped and peered through the wide gap in the doorway because Casper didn't lend himself complete privacy. She saw a portion of glass, however, the width didn't span the distance for her to identify his nude impression since the majority of the shower was secreted behind the door closed halfway. Realistically, she wouldn't have seen him anyway due to heated moisture spreading a thick film on the interior glass. Running water was all that she could distinguish, along with the bloodstained shirt upon the rest of his dirty laundry on the floor.

She crept into the hallway, careful not to cause a disturbance that would summon his attention on her path of exploration. The continuous hiss of water jetting from the faucet loudened along the way. Finally, she reached the door - pushing it open and exposing a full view of the bathroom. His bleared image writhed as he showered beyond the glass.

She entered the room. Now up close, she still

wasn't able to see him clearly through streaks of smog. Reminiscing his touch, while recollecting how protective he professed himself to be over her, intensified romantic thirsts that she felt she must surrender.

She grabbed the bottom of her large, baggy shirt and pulled it up and over her head, cleansing her chest from fabric. After dropping the shirt next to his filthy attire, she slipped her thumbs into the waistband on the sides of her hips and thrust the sweatpants down to her ankles. The forbidden region between her thighs was bare since she wasn't given a pair of clean panties to put on following her shower yesterday evening. That neglected area was responsible for guiding her to the glass door, because it hungered for attention. Much anticipation between her legs convinced her that the warm flesh was on the verge of salivating.

She opened the door on the glass enclosure and the first thing she saw was Casper's broad backside. His shoulders were herculean compared to the average guy. Her first instinct was to visualize herself incapable of getting her arms all of the way around him during an intimate embrace.

Allowing her eyes to trek slowly down his hindside, Shei made out that his thick and seemingly firm buttocks were a few shades lighter than his back and legs. The lighter tone stretched halfway down the back of his thighs before the skin darkened again. She couldn't help but take another glimpse at his ass. There was plenty of meat on both cheeks for her to get those small hands on and squeeze. Imagining how a moment in his arms might unfold was beginning to work her up; she noticed the struggle to breathe ordinarily was progressing, and the urge to touch him became increasingly unbearable to withstand.

She stepped inside the walk-in shower, never once taking her eyes off him.

Casper must have heard the magnet catch when the door sealed the enclosure because he spun around, covering his penis behind both hands, with his eyes enlarged almost as wide as the alarm-stricken opening between his lips.

Water surging over him melted shampoo down his face before it trickled upon his chest and continued a long, messy path to his stomach. Shei glimpsed at his hands, probably hoping to see a little something but he was totally sheltered. Then she looked into his eyes once more, and smirked.

He focused on her eyes, also. Not once did he draw away and take advantage of reveling in the view of bare breasts, or any other places on her body that may entice persuasion.

"What the hell are you doing?" he asked, wavering in surprise.

She took a step closer, losing control of her flirtatious grin as the rapacity to cease resistance entered upon devouring abstinence. His unusual perseverance confirmed that he had not experienced sensual activity for quite some time.

"You told me to come if I needed you, so I came," she whispered, provocatively. Then she reached out and placed one hand on his slick chest, before adding, "Not really, but that's why I'm here."

He sucked back mumbling indistinctly, which she thought involved getting caught off guard more than it dealt with him being nervous. Casper might be a large, visually powerful man, but his impactful sensitivity to expressing prudence barred any degree of intimidation that she should feel toward him.

"Have you lost your mind? You don't want to get mixed up with me. I'm not what you've been missing," he said.

"I know what you are," she breathed, inching forward and pressing her small breasts on top of his washboard abdomen. "You're better than what you give yourself credit for. If you were convicted of something you didn't do, then it shouldn't neglect the person you were before the fact."

"People have always treated me like I did it. I don't know how else to react," he confessed.

Shei slid her hand from his chest and went all of the way up and over his shoulder. She arched her head back and narrowed her eyes, as if inviting him to lean down and embrace her. "React how your mind is telling you. What do you want? Do you want to get looked at negatively and pushed aside, or do you want to step up to the plate and take a chance on everything you've been denied?"

He expelled a gust of frustration. "I don't know. I just think that getting involved with me isn't best for you."

"Mmm. Did you not save my life? Have you not treated me how I've always wished a man would?" she inquired, preserving her delicate tone.

He chuckled. "Yeah, but it doesn't mean you've got to give me anything. Especially like this."

She tilted her head to one side, lengthening her vulnerable neck. "I wouldn't suggest that you think of it as me offering you something. I'd like to think we're two adults in the position to enjoy what it is we want at the moment."

He felt her enticing tone claw at his thoughts. Her disrobed flesh squeezing against him didn't help to stave off thinking inappropriately. The long existent eye contact that he somehow managed to maintain suddenly disintegrated when he glimpsed at the exaggerated upwards bulge in her breasts, resulting from them being mashed against him.

Shei giggled. "I don't know about you but I find this way better than what we're supposed to be doing. Sure you want to pass on the opportunity?"

Something inside of him, teeming with instinct, took over without Casper giving it much consideration. He removed his hands from in front of him, at least one of them that she was aware of, and reached up behind her before weaving her hair around it. Once it was all wrapped around and his hand pressed her skull, he jerked her head up straight and yanked backwards for her chin to point at him.

A moment ago she wasn't sure what happened with his other hand, but she was quickly made aware when it grabbed around her throat. He squeezed until she gasped, choking. Shei didn't know if he intended to apply violent pressure; however, since his disputable background did portray the bad boy persona, she assumed that such intensity was in his substance. In the past, she would voice her opinion in retaliation against a man getting too physical. What she wished to experience with Casper was an irregular desire, consisting of wholly submitting herself while undergoing assertive treatment. She believed that getting sternly dominated would cause her to feel safeguarded. After yesterday and this evening, she needed to witness that he was in control because she was on the cusp of having a total meltdown.

He relieved just a fraction of the pressure around her throat. Fortunately, she could breathe now - with difficulty still - and gasped, wheezing. Casper didn't speak. He did not have to utter one word, honestly. A dim gleam in his eyes hinted at mystification which she was convinced had fractured his stability.

His motive was not to instill fear, yet he distinguished mild unease looking up at him. Not really sure about how to deal with her, he pulled away from gripping her neck and stepped back. Creating distance gave him the opportunity to brush his explorative fingers along a broader region. Instead of devouring one breast with a firm grip, he swiped down its side and then rubbed underneath. Along the way, he stretched his thumb over the nipple and pressed as his fingers maneuvered toward the center of her chest. Following this gentle outline, he extended his extra-large hand on the breast and squeezed unemphatically.

She groaned.

She shut her eyes and snarled her lips, as fierce treatment escalated to almost becoming intolerable. Obviously, he was inexperienced in handling women since he was mindless about providing momentary discomfort. Regardless of how much pain she received, Shei was not going to urge him to stop. Strangely, she identified herself yearning for more inadvertent punishment. His profound method of dealing with her ravaged the regret and despair she suffered for her involvement in Elliot's murder. Furthermore, she sensed Casper's assertive edge react as a bandaid, temporarily overlaying resentment toward her disloyal father.

He pulled her breast before bringing his fingers together and pinching the nipple. Then he let go completely, and scraped down her stomach. He continued bearing down upon her skin until reaching beneath her bellybutton at which point he laid his hand flat and sailed between her legs. Since a handful of years had passed after he last had any sort of relations with a woman, he didn't exactly sink into prodding her with pleasantry.

She twitched and pivoted her hips when his middle finger drove inside of her without taking the time to enchantingly massage her sensitive region beforehand. His internal digging was so discomforting that she broke skin with her nails when curling her fingers on his shoulder.

"Ehh," she hissed, bowing her forehead on his chest.

Casper thrust his finger as deep as it could go ahead of turning his hand so that the side of his finger applied pressure against one of her vagina's interior walls. He withdrew slowly, bringing the back end of his fingernail to the opening. Suddenly, he rammed into her again - all at once.

"Oh!" she moaned, prying her nails even further into his shoulder. "Oh my god!"

Witnessing the inevitable rapture of ecstasy inundate her existence was all that it took to establish the foundation for him to intensify erogenous aspirations. He devoted more energy to pulling her hair which tugged her head further backwards until her entire face aimed at the ceiling.

Infatuation-

Appetency-

Erotomania-

Casper leaned down and touched her lips. His mouth consumed hers entirely, giving him the dominant advantage to control both of their moves while indulging the breath stained flavor of her mouth's moist flesh. He broke away from the taste and dragged the underside of his tongue along her chin before gliding beneath her face to luxuriate in the length of neck awaiting euphoric delirium.

Keeping her one hand on his shoulder, Shei reached between them with the other and apprehended his cock from dangling freely between them. Despite it not being firm due to bending every time she yanked forward, she still considered that it might be the largest she fumbled upon. Its girth certainly outdistanced her past experiences. The maximum length hadn't been achieved but she was working diligently to get it there.

While he persisted in holding her head back and pursued lipping every inch of her neck, Casper succumbed to the unfamiliarity of her hand being not his own jerking him off. He became solid; so much adrenaline gushed throughout his penis that he perceived its veins pounding against those fingers gripping tightly.

Shei groaned, stroking him harder. She felt the finger inside her rub back and forth with ease now, because the length of his erection caused an unprecedented craving which made her wet in places the water didn't touch. As expected, he was incredibly endowed. Far larger than other penises that she had mistakenly allowed inside.

"I want you," she expired.

"Yeah?" he asked, panting against her neck.

"Yeah. Like right now," she made clear. "Don't make me wait anymore."

He removed his vaginal juice wrinkled finger out from between her legs and let go of holding her hair. Then he pulled away from her neck and looked down, seeing the strain in facial muscles as she prolonged jerking him with determination that he remain hard.

"Dammit. You make that feel good," he gasped.

"Might feel better if you helped us both out," she whispered, finally opening her eyes to him while lingering lost in ideas about degrees of titillation she might endure if he hurried and had his way with her.

Casper snagged her hips and spun the two of them around, picking her up and slamming her against the wall like one hundred and twenty-two pounds wasn't anything to him. To prevent falling, she wrapped one leg around his side and lugged her heel on the top of his buttocks. He hoisted the other leg against his opposite side and curled his arm under the bend in her knee, utilizing it as a brace to avert her from slipping in the event things got too intense. Shei also helped uphold her weight by reaching both arms around the back of his broad neck.

Getting inside of her included overcoming minimal difficulty, and Casper didn't know if the reason pertained to him being too thick or if it resulted from Shei not having sex for so long that his attempt basically amounted to her losing her virginity all over again. After a few pokes on the two smooth, hairless folds, he felt himself nudge the warm center.

Shei tightened her entire body and winced at the moment he stuffed every throbbing inch of his hurtful cock into the depth of her.

"Oh fuck! God!" she wailed painfully, almost crying.

A slow and sympathetic rhythm would have been logical following insertion but Casper showed no concern for treating her gently. He rammed insensately against her, time and again, treating her like an effigy getting jabbed with a needle.

"Uah! Uah! Uahh-" she moaned, shutting her eyes and resting her head on the wall to prevent unintentionally striking it while in the act.

Unsurprisingly, she couldn't produce any other sounds between the quick, repetitive jarring of her body, and she was okay with that.

Shei was getting exactly what she wanted.

What had been missing for way too long.

If there was one thing she learned, then it was the knowledge that the long-established *size doesn't matter* proclamation amongst women was a myth. Size really did matter. The botheration derived from extensive pleasure was indiscriminately profound, however, she wouldn't have accepted it any other way. This abusive conduct really did prove itself triumphant in banishing all recent negativities from her mind.

Casper was displaced from registering their prior disturbances, too. Shei's fingernails dug so far into him that the scratches should have been stinging, but he didn't apprehend pain either. His only focus was to give her the utmost satisfaction, and so far she gave the impression that he was navigating the task excellently. Things between them may have started out with her crotch feeling as dry as the Atacama, yet after several violent thrusts, she presented him with the anomalous idea of how it might feel if he shoved his cock into a microwaved cantaloupe.

Slish.

Slosh.

The sound of his cock driving through her secretion became louder than water gushing down from overhead, but it could not compare to the voluminous echo bouncing all around as their bodies clapped together. Each thrust sent her riding up the wall, and letting out the same relishable groan.

With their shared desire discharging messily from one body to the next, it was apparent that they had found something in each other more valuable than the bloodshed they were recruited to perform.

When Shei believed there was nothing left within herself to excrete, he intensified his erratic motions, straining every drop of juice that she didn't think remained.

Casper's own built up formula released and burst inside her. She likely felt the dose of warm jizz splatter throughout her anatomy, because she leaned forward and laid her head on the side of his face. Hyperventilating in his ear, although she hadn't done much to debilitate her stamina, Shei lowered the one leg that he wasn't cradling. This obviously indicated that she was incapable of repeating the session consecutively. His reaction, though, differed from her signal to disconnect. Not only did Casper maintain the grip on her leg, but he kept up pushing inside her, too.

The hurt prolonged by his uninterrupted craze wasn't sustainable anymore. This sense that she was being split ached and spread unsettling pressure between her legs.

"I can't anymore," she alleged, decimated by his release of long suppressed sexual tension.

"Shh. You don't need to do anything. Just go with my flow," he insisted, before raising his hand and combing through her hair.

His pace changed abruptly once he recognized distress, switching from fast and reckless to slow and considerate. The ease in penetrating her remained steady since a couple of effective orgasms creamed his shaft only a short while ago. Revising his rhythm was incapable of altering the outcome at this point; Shei felt pain just in their continuous contact alone.

"This isn't going to work. I'm- I-" A deeply unsettling growl quashed what she was trying to say. "Fuck!" she roared.

Casper ran his fingers up the back of her head, clenching a handful of hair before yanking her head back and pressing his hand on the wall. He turned and brushed his nose along the side of her neck, sneaking toward her ear, where he paused and reached his tongue on the bottom hindside of the earlobe. Following a quick lick, he leaned further and bit gently.

Under ordinary circumstances, Shei would have been driven wild getting her ear nibbled, however, persistent botheration turned casual pleasure into pure hell. She pulled her head slightly, enough to separate his teeth from snaring her flesh. While his habitual intrusion between her thighs was the epicenter for agony, she did not attempt to push him away and end the hysteria.

He kissed the rear side of her jaw in front of her ear. "I've never felt anyone this good. I can't get enough of you," he whispered.

She turned and kissed the side of his face like he did to her. "Well, I've never had someone want me so badly. It's flattering to know I've still got a little something."

"More than a little," he assured.

"Mmmm," she expressed, bowing her forehead upon his shoulder.

He reached down and grabbed the thigh of the leg hanging between him and the wall. He lifted it around his hip, securing it the way he did the other one still wrapped around his side. Then he stopped thrusting and shoved himself against her helpless body, preserving his placement inside her.

"I don't know what you do to me," he said, breathing heavily.

She uncurled her fingers from sinking their nails into his shoulder and slipped lower, patting his back. "I'm not sure either, but I am definitely not opposed to finding out."

They stood motionless beneath the water raging down on them like violent rain battering rocks. Each fought to conquer their fatigued vitality and overcome difficulty breathing. The spillage of ecstasy which bound them together remained warm, enshrouding their distant parts with extended delectation. Though it was apparent that they had aborted insistent starvation, there was still an

immaterial obsession that denied either of them the decency
to seek desertion.

CHAPTER NINETEEN

She turned sideways, evading light that touched annoyingly upon her eyelids, and stretched out her arm. All that she felt was a large bare space on the bed. Opening her eyes, she was shocked to discover that Casper neglected her. After last night, she was convinced that their unusual alliance was beginning to convert into an enchanting connection. She went to bed forfeiting her emotional wall, because he held her much tighter and more meaningfully than the night prior.

Disappointment jolted her upright.

Out of all her newfound expectations, lonesomeness wasn't one of them.

She pulled the blanket aside and rushed off the bed. Storming across the bedroom as if her life depended on it, she blazed through the doorway since Casper obviously failed closing the door every time he left the room. She stopped at the bannister and peered over the living room. The television was off and there was no sign of him. To the right of the television was the broken window with a gray bed sheet spread across the vastly damaged lower portion. She couldn't see what held the sheet in place but assumed that he must have found some thumbtacks somewhere and pinned it in place since both sides stretched onto the walls beyond the window casing.

Looking directly below the balcony, Shei glimpsed at the portion of the island visible to her. For a moment, she wondered if he might be making breakfast but she didn't see or hear any commotion.

Turning in the direction of the staircase, she noticed the door to the first bedroom on the right was open. Peering inside, she saw the bed had been downgraded to just its two pillows and bare mattress on the frame. There was no doubt that he robbed the bed of its sheet and comforter in order to conceal the shattered window, however, the blanket wasn't suspended against the glass. Actually, she didn't recall seeing it anywhere.

"Hey! Where are you?!" she hollered, crossing the short distance and jogging down the stairs.

She landed upon the downstairs flooring and stalled at once. A slim feeling of hope encouraged her to suppose that he might be taking a shower first thing in the morning. Unfortunately, that trace amount of optimism evaporated the moment she looked to the end of the hall and saw the bathroom door standing wide open. If he was in the shower, then she would have heard water flowing from where she was standing; also, his smudgy impression would be distinguishable within smog on the glass. What she saw was a crystal clear encasement, providing her with the view of a dry and empty interior.

"Well, where the fuck is he?" she asked herself.

Twisting toward the kitchen, Shei was confronted by the most atrocious display without even having to step forward. The walkway dividing the island from the stovetop and sink area was obstructed by a hefty lump of gray comforter. Finally, the blanket taken from the bedroom had been detected. Its unusual shape left nothing for her imagination to speculate, because the length and width of the object hidden underneath perfectly matched the dimensions of a human body.

Discomfort.

Sorrow.

Fear.

Every negative emotion that Casper cleansed from her mind suddenly regenerated, now twice as intense for the reason that she was alone. No degree of all the pleasant sensations that he caused her to experience existed any longer. Terror and anxiety reigned inside her so much that she felt their unfavorable influence ground her in place. She wanted to proceed and find Casper, but animosity toward what lay ahead weighed heavily on that aspiration.

Confusedness scrambled her ability to think clearly. On top of things beginning to not make sense. She didn't know anything about Elliot, including his name, and it puzzled her to not know his reason for targeting them. Regrettably, the ultimate uncertainty troubling her was why Casper up and left without giving notice. Now, she felt that she'd been taken for a fool - used to satisfy the needs that no sensible woman would entertain.

Nervousness over isolation provoked a sporadic heartbeat, and her hands began to tremble constantly. Suddenly, she was short winded and struggling in every effort to catch her breath. Lastly, she recognized that her face was clammy and flooded with sweat after reaching up and touching her forehead in response to stress.

Despite this nasty panic attack far removing her from the joyful mindset she was thrown into last night, she mustered the courage to go forward. Having a corpse as her only companion intensified eeriness in the atmosphere coming at her from all around. She stopped just a few steps inside the kitchen and looked into the living room again, seeing everything still as they were when she stared down from the balcony. What little hope remained that she might find Casper situated someplace not in her recent view quickly perished upon determining that he wasn't anywhere.

She glanced at the enshrouded cadaver. Disbelief that she played a role in committing murder was sort of fresh, and led her to understand that she would not have had the ability to kill Casper if things had gone down like originally designed.

Looking away from the covered window to glimpse at the refrigerator and then back at the window again, she gathered the impression that she was indisputably ignorant about how her situation would unfold from this moment onwards. Her survival decimated the outcome everyone expected, however, since no one involved was aware of the circumstance, she assumed that her father was eagerly awaiting to prepare funeral arrangements. Additionally, the greedy bastard was possibly collecting all the proper documentation to hurry and replace her name with his own on the trust set up for Sierra.

Continuing to scour her surroundings, Shei identified something that wasn't present last night or any time prior. Laying on the island was a cellular phone with a small square piece of yellow paper beneath it. With curiosity mounting to get the best of her, she rushed alongside the island to check what she believed Casper left for her to run across. The phone was not one that she recognized, and she definitely didn't know anyone who carried such an older flip-style model. She couldn't make out the cellular provider's name because the white lettering was practically rubbed off the blue paint. Evidently this device had outlived multiple upgrade eligibilities, if it still functioned.

Without wasting another second marveling over something considered antique nowadays, she nudged the phone aside to check the note. The message read:

Hey Girl,

Call your father, first thing. Act cool and tell him the job is done. Tell him that you took care of me and the other guy. Don't stress yourself over anything else. I know what needs to be done. I'll explain.

Shei sighed, fretting over calling her father regardless of what the letter requested. His role as the kingpin of scheduling his own daughter's execution infuriated her, and she wasn't positive that she could calmly play along and give the impression that everything was okay while pretending to not know how things were actually supposed to unfold. But the realization nagged her that communication must be made, or else he'd suspect something was amidst the bedlam and resort to handling the matter by other means.

She picked up the phone.

Flipped it open.

The background on the screen was clotted by multiple icons but appeared to display a handgun alongside a line of suspected cocaine on a small wooden table top. She goggled at the screen for a moment, trying to remember her father's phone number. All that came to mind was *Asshole (Dad)* - his *Contact* name that showed whenever she made an outgoing call to him, or displayed every time he reached out to her.

She tapped the *Contacts* icon and a slew of alphabetized names popped up. Since the first seventeen letters didn't mean anything to her, she scrolled quickly down the list and breached the *N*'s before landing instantly upon the *R*'s; therefore, there were just fourteen letters bypassed, according to this particular list.

Reading carefully through every last name that started with *R*, she found the holy grail - *Rivera* - near the bottom and pressed the *OK* button surrounded by four directional keys. Suddenly, the names list was replaced by contact information for Rivera. Having no interest in any basic data about him, Shei struck the green dash at the top far left side of the dial pad.

The screen switched to a faceless *Contact* image.

She pushed the button displaying a speakerphone symbol and a continuous ringing sound blared out into the room.

She gasped.

Preserved her breath.

A billow of dread overcame her, more powerfully than the agitation which infested her thoughts after finding that she was truly abandoned.

Finally, she exhaled - contemplating all the potential

uncertainties that may arise at the moment he answered.

Liam Rivera had just finalized and submitted an email to an attorney, concerning a defendant's request to enter into a six month program of addiction recovery as a form of plea agreement, when his cellular phone began ringing.

He reached across the left side of the desk and snatched the phone laying on a thin pile of loose papers. Bringing it forward, he looked at the screen and saw the name *Elliot*. Beneath the name was a phone number. Right away, pride in the form of tingling warmth cascaded upon him because he speculated this call was the one to inform him that the obligation was consummated.

He brushed his thumb along the screen, accepting the call.

The line silenced.

Liam smirked arrogantly. He waited a long time for this occasion to come to fruition. "I imagine that you've got wondrous news for me this morning?" he asked, tilting back in his seat and kicking one leg up on the desk before raising the other and crossing it on top of the first one. "Come on now. Tell me how it went. I want details."

"I did as you asked," mentioned a calm, low voice.

The shockingly unexpected, soft voice peeled back his eyelids with disbelief. "Shei," he uttered, almost breathlessly. "Sweetheart, how did everything turn out?"

"Well, I've got that wondrous news for you this morning. I took care of that dude like you wanted me to do. Oddly, someone else must have been involved because another guy showed up, but I handled that situation also.

Why didn't you inform me that I'd have company? I wasn't aware that I'd have to do the job twice," she specified.

Liam coughed, and scratched his face nervously. "Umm. Darling, I did advise someone to sort of step in and ghost you. In case you weren't capable of handling the responsibility on your own, then I had someone willing to take over. However, it sounds to me that you've taken care of the matter and then some. I would have had him dealt with anyway, because anyone knowing outside of me and you is, realistically, one too many."

"Okay. So, who's going to clean up this mess?" she inquired.

He sighed, leaned his head back on the cushion, and stared at the ceiling - plotting what to say before relaying the message. "Just you leave that to me. I've got a few guys that owe me a favor."

"How many people are you involved with, exactly?" she asked.

He spun his chair halfway and faced the window. "The number of people in my corner isn't the point. All that matters is who I'm involved with will continue to disassociate your name with all this."

"Okay," she said softly.

He withdrew his feet off the desk and leaned forward, planting one elbow on the table while holding the phone against his ear. He was thoroughly impressed by the mood within their conversation because he supposed that if she suspected anything, then he'd recognize nervousness in her tone. Her voice would tremble, and she'd likely be skittish with words.

Maintaining invisibility amongst his worries was

difficult, though, since she annihilated every expectation he envisioned for the rest of his life. "Want me to come or send someone to get you?" he asked.

She considered multiple scenarios and the one that stuck with her pertained to someone being sent to pick her up but with no intent to take her home. Her father hired a man to murder her and common sense pointed out the fact that he'd probably assign the task to whoever was next in line to return a favor. He knew too many roughnecks on the wrong side of the law. They all were the type of person that could make an individual disappear and the body never be recovered.

"Nah. I'm going to straighten the place up some. I'll be in touch after a while," she said.

"Shei," he fired back abruptly, "you don't have to touch anything. I've got a few people that are going to erase every trace of what's happened."

"They can come in behind me, but I'm going to make sure for myself that I've left no evidence of me being here," she stated.

"Very well," he responded, twisting his chair forward and facing the desk. "Do what you feel is necessary. Once you think things are satisfactory, then call me back and I'll send someone in a hurry."

"Yeah-" Shei breathed into the phone. "I'm sure that you can't wait to send somebody to my rescue. Must be nice having so many people willing to do so much for you. You piece together this perfect arrangement and everyone steps up to the plate, ready to get their hands dirty. I'll be in touch."

"I'm always looking out for your best interests. Do

what you've got-" Liam paused, and listened to the dial tone blare loud in his ear. He wasn't surprised that she hung up on him because it was what she did every time she got aggravated - which didn't happen often, however, when she did fall into one of these ill moods, he knew to pull away and allow her time to calm down because she always came back to daddy.

Thinking that this was just another basic episode involving her aggravation, he set the phone on the desk without botheration. Perhaps she convinced him in his own deceitful game that the true nature overshadowing the situation was not suspected.

Then again, Liam did have a collective of individuals prepared to do his bidding; maybe he didn't feel agitated since what was supposed to have been done could still be fulfilled in secrecy amongst his inner circle.

Shei slung the phone on the island, pressed both hands on her hips, and arched her head straight back. She could not fathom the amount of anxiety that inconvenienced her when on the phone. Every second, she worried that she might expose the combination of dread and discomfort. It required extreme willpower to prevent her voice from cracking and shedding light on the fact that not everything was okay. She struggled so much to keep it all together that she was gasping for air after getting off the phone.

Suddenly, she felt two large hands grab the back of her arms.

She tensed.

All that she could think about was this being the

final seconds of her life. The ultimate dread set in that her father sent someone to make certain the job had been completed prior to speaking with her.

There was so much unexpected anguish that she felt a lone tear sneak out of her eye and roll down her face.

Whoever had this firm grip, made a quick move that turned her away from facing the kitchen and forced her to confront them. Her heart sank during the time that she was being spun around, however, it stopped descending once she got a clear visual of the individual steering her.

Looking down, Casper sneered and released her arms. "Did you seriously think I'd leave you behind?"

She swallowed the hollow mouthful of temporary despair. "I did! When I saw the phone and note, I thought that was it…convinced me that you'd fled, and I was alone to figure the rest of this shit out on my own."

He reached up and swiped the back of one hand down the side of her face. "I wouldn't do that to you. This situation is too big and stretches beyond the here and now. I'm sure there's already a plan for when you go back. Probably rig your murder to resemble an accident. Even if things didn't look right, it would result in a botched investigation. They're clever, and well connected."

"Oh, I know. He asked if I wanted someone to pick me up," she stated.

"What did you say?" he fired back.

"Pretty much, I bought us some time. Told him I was going to clear my tracks. Unfortunately, I know he's probably going to send somebody anyway, so we've got to act fast," she replied.

He withdrew from touching her face and scratched

underneath his nose. "We've got wheels. Dude's car is just up the road. Can't be running around in it for too long, though. I'm sure those plates are going to be on everyone's radar."

She nodded in agreement. "Okay. We've just got to run by the school and pick up my daughter. I'm not giving him any opportunity to get to her first. After that, I don't care what you do with the vehicle. I've got my own."

"You know what has to be done, right?" he asked.

"What do you mean?" she inquired, rumpling her brows confusedly.

He grabbed the bill of his ole dirty hat and lifted it slightly, offering her a better view of those majestic eyes. "He's going to come for you until someone stops him. I know he's your father and all, but this isn't something that ends with a hug and apology. Realistically, it comes down to you or him. One of you isn't going to make it through."

"So what are you getting at?" she asked.

He frowned just shortly. "There's only one way to stop him, and I think you know what that entails."

"You're saying I should kill him?" she continued questioning.

"If you don't do something, then I can guarantee you that something will be done to you," he answered directly.

Everything about her demeanor shifted drastically. Her shoulders slumped, and she lowered her head and eyed the floor for a moment. When she did look up at him again, she repetitively scanned his eyes with hopes of discovering something she couldn't quite comprehend. All of her anxiety multiplied. She felt it increase so much that it initiated her gut feeling of wanting to vomit.

"I can't!" she exclaimed nervously. "There's got to be another way."

Recognizing her unease, he reached out and grasped her hips gently, sympathizing with her like he had done during the past two nights. He maintained unwavering eye contact while pulling her toward him slowly.

"I'm not asking you to do anything. Get your daughter and go home. Wait for me there. I'll take care of what needs to be done," he assured.

"I can't stand back and let you go to that extreme. You're talking about the death penalty," she said.

He pressed hard on her hip bones. "Nobody is going to do anything. They all know we know they're involved, so no one is going to raise a finger and get themselves in the middle of all this because they know I've got enough information to dirty their names."

"I don't know. This is way too dangerous," she stressed.

"This is your freedom. Also, it's a decision that will preserve your daughter's future well-being," he mentioned.

Shei sighed. She'd become sincerely stressed in dealing with increased aggravation. "He's my father, and all that I've got other than Sierra."

"You've got me," he confessed, before removing one hand off her hip and reaching her face to glide his thumb across her lips. "And he isn't your father anymore. That man is your death certificate. I will not let you place yourself in harm's way by allowing him to walk freely. I am going to do something about it, regardless of whether you like it or not."

"I don't want-"

Her vocal defense became disrupted when Casper bent down and smashed his lips upon her own. It wasn't the deeply passionate type like he gave her in the shower, however, it was spontaneous and meaningful enough to distract her brain and all prior emotions. The nagging urge to vomit turned to butterflies in her stomach. Shei was consumed entirely by uplifting sentiments, but she didn't want to express herself out of fear that all of this would be nothing more than a short lived experience. Since none of her past romantic involvements blossomed into anything exceptional, she sensed no reason to jump the gun and assume this wonderful encounter might escalate to greater things.

Just when it felt like the situation was deepening, he pulled back entirely.

Shei found herself unable to breathe because his delicate affection hypothetically sucked life from her. Even her eyes remained closed - adding insult to injury.

Casper studied her intently while grazing his fingers down the back on one side of her face. "I got you, and for as long as I've got any say in the matter, I'll not let anyone endanger you and your daughter."

CHAPTER TWENTY

Once he slowed on the road and made a turn onto the driveway, Liam discovered something that engulfed him in dismay. Beatrice's vehicle was gone, which he considered to be rather odd, because she'd always pick up Sierra at school and then return to wait for him to arrive home after work. The lone vehicle awaiting him belonged to Elliot. Of course, he was well aware that Elliot met a grim fate and was not the person at his house.

He crept and parked alongside the vehicle before noticing there wasn't anyone occupying it. "What a fucking mess," he complained under his breath, presuming that Shei had gone into the house and was with Sierra.

The fact that she didn't listen really pissed him off. He had a strong backup plan since the initial one fell through. All that he would've had to do was speed dial another pathetic felon that owed him a huge favor, and everything would have worked out. Shei would have been off guard and under the impression that someone was being sent to pick her up, while Liam sat back and anxiously awaited the phone call to inform him that she was no longer a burden. Everything was well orchestrated and supposed to be executed proficiently, but things went south once and then again. Ultimately, Liam realized that it was up to only him to perpetrate corruption. He wasn't exactly prepared to murder his own daughter, but two million dollars on his mind did provoke the willful aspiration.

"If you want something done, you've got to do it yourself. Never fails," he mumbled, snatching his small work briefcase off the passenger seat and then exiting the vehicle.

He nudged the door shut and gave Elliot's car a brief glimpse. He didn't glance at it under the assumption something may have miraculously appeared after the first time he looked. Liam examined the automobile briefly due to anger of it being there.

After crossing the lawn, climbing the steps, and reaching the house, he was a bit stumped upon finding the door locked. Shei knew what time he got home from work because she often dropped off Sierra at that hour, whenever she had personal matters to conduct. He didn't think too much about it, though, since Beatrice was always at the house when she came around. She did just survive a near fatal abduction. Perhaps locking the door was a subconscious gesture of botheration she suffered from the ordeal.

Liam unlocked the door.

Opened it.

Peered across the long depth of his quiet home.

Ordinarily, Sierra would come running to greet him as soon as he set both feet inside the house. Oddly, that wasn't the case today. Since the home was unusually peaceful, it was impossible that neither Shei or Sierra didn't hear him enter. He didn't get the sneaking suspicion that Shei knew what was going on, but things just didn't feel right.

"Sweetheart?!" he yelled, closing and locking the door. "I see you've made it in one piece!"

Ongoing silence was all that continued to provide companionship.

"Shei?!" he called out, setting his briefcase on the small oval table below the five-peg coat rack mounted diagonally on the wall.

Still, he got no response.

"Sierra?!" he spoke up in the kindest voice possible.

Nothing.

Even the casual patter of little feet storming throughout the house failed to register.

Stepping to the large entryway leading into the living room, he peered across the unoccupied space and saw the light and television both were off.

Where the hell can they be?, he wondered.

He turned toward the second large entryway behind him and checked the dining area. That room, too, was dark and void of life.

There was only one other place they could be. Upstairs. In Sierra's newly renovated permanent bedroom. Maybe she was showing her mother all of the latest additions; walls coated with week old purple paint, brand new *Princess* bed, and superhero display case to brandish all of her *Marvel* action figures. Sierra was ecstatic about these wonderful accessories her pawpaw included to make the bedroom more homely, so it made sense that she was probably advertising it to her mother.

He walked gracefully toward the staircase just a short distance beyond where he stood between entryways. He breached the bottom step-

"They're not here," stated a male voice.

Liam hesitated going any farther, and looked alongside the staircase to glare at the doorway to the kitchen ahead. "Who are you?!" he asked demandingly.

"Come on, Liam. Let's not play dumb with each other. You know who it is," the voice replied.

Descending off the steps and trudging aside, Liam looked a little harder to see if he could make out anyone standing in the part of the kitchen visible to him. He didn't see the man but knew that he was there, somewhere, because it's where the voice was coming from.

"Floyd, is that you?!" Liam asked.

The man laughed while staying out of view.

Liam stood up straight, crossed his arms on his chest, and frowned with dissatisfaction. "What are you doing here?! I was told that you'd been taken care of. You're supposed to be dead."

"I was dealt with, all right. But I can promise you that it was in ways you don't want to hear," the voice pledged.

Casper Floyd emerged from behind the side of the doorway and stopped in the center of the opening. He faced Liam. A stark grin stretched across his face, and those eyes which Shei thought were marvelous suddenly winced in representation of something dull and vile. The caring, considerate man that he had expressed himself to be seemed to quickly become replaced by an individual bent on creating insensitive chaos.

"Let's talk about something. Help me make sense of the situation," he said, taking a step forward inside the foyer. "You got me involved because you wanted your daughter dismissed so that everything in your big scheme of things would work just the way you envisioned. But then, you went behind my back and devised this other plan for her to off me. You never change, do you? Always going to be that piece of shit that'll doublecross somebody just to make certain everything goes his way. Doesn't matter who's involved, you've always got some type of bullshit up your sleeve."

Liam uncrossed his arms from the confrontational stance, and smiled. "Allow me to explain. I gave my daughter the order because it was the only way she'd get involved. I needed for her to be comfortable walking into this situation. One minor fuck up and she might have suspected something; so I did what I-"

"You did fuck up," Casper interrupted. "You sent some other piece of shit to take out me and your daughter. You had your own plan all along. You wanted us to go at it, hoping one of us would get pulverized, and then have someone else come in and tidy up all of the loose ends. You thought you were pretty clever. I do give you credit, though. It probably could have worked."

Liam smirked, and chuckled. "Seriously, you have no idea what the hell you are talking about. You wouldn't be standing here right now if I wanted you killed. Tell me, have you forgotten who you're talking to?"

"Oh, nah. I know exactly who I'm speaking with. The same man that did everything in his power to make damn sure that I was the one who took the fall when Dillon hit that kid. You and Alfonso both knew I didn't do shit. Hell, Dillon even came out and admitted that he was the one driving, but you didn't do a damn thing with that information. Instead, you had him lie under oath, made it out that I was the one behind the wheel, and got me locked up while Dillon didn't have to endure any of the legal repercussions. Yeah, Liam, I most definitely know who you are," Casper acknowledged.

"Jesus Christ. Get over the past, would you? Dillon had a lot going for him, and Alfonso didn't want to watch it all get pissed down the drain over some unfortunate mishap. Yeah, maybe what I did wasn't ethical, but it seemed like the right thing to do at the moment. Everyone played a unique role in how things panned out. None of us were innocent, actually. But all of that is behind us now. We've moved on," Liam expressed.

Casper shook his head disapprovingly. "You call Dillon killing himself moving on? He couldn't deal with shit because of you and Alfonso shoving everything under the rug."

Liam sighed. "I'm an attorney, not a therapist. I can't fix whatever fucked up shit is going on inside someone's head. I did him a favor and the fact that he couldn't handle it was on him."

"You're just a pure asshole," Casper mentioned, snarling his face at him. "I lost years of my life over the crap you pulled. I can't get that time back. You ruined my reputation. People are always talking shit and thinking that I'm everything I'm not. No one will give me the time of day."

Liam slipped one hand in the front pocket of his slacks. "I did offer restitution for your hardships. Screw what people think about you. Most of the time, those individuals that consider themselves better are much worse pieces of shit. Fifteen thousand dollars, on the other hand, could have done you some good. Just one simple task was all that you had to do, and I'd taken care of you. But as usual, you've chosen to make things difficult."

Casper took a couple of steps forward before stopping and pointing a finger at him. "Don't act like you were paying for my struggles. You wanted me to murder someone for that money."

Liam giggled, and withdrew his hand from the pocket. "Doesn't matter why you would've got the money. What's important is that it would have made everything you've gone through feel worthwhile."

"You make it sound like fifteen grand should be life changing for a man like myself," Casper said, after initially responding with sarcastic laughter. "I'll tell you right now, your money doesn't mean anything to me. I've got what I need to change direction. I'm sure Alfonso informed you of the diary Dillon kept. I bet he told you that it was in a safe place, too. Truth is, I've got it. I'm going to bring the system down and everyone's going with it. Sure, I'll win some big lawsuit in the end, but exposing all of the lies and constant corruption is worth far more than anything you could offer."

Sudden tension prompted Liam to make a fist with his hand at his side, however, he abstained from signaling directional aggression. "I wouldn't recommend anyone make such foolish threats. We are a powerful group of people. Isn't difficult to deal with someone and no one knows what happened. Having that inside knowledge yourself, you know how quickly we're capable of causing an inconvenience," he boasted arrogantly.

Casper smirked. "I'm not threatening anyone. I'm telling you what I am going to do. In addition, your daughter is off limits. I cannot let you do what you've got in mind. She doesn't deserve it. All that she's been dealt her whole life is misfortune. Frankly, having you as a father is the worst of all things."

Liam drew his mouth tight and gnawed the bottom lip. "How dare you insult me like this. Remember where you came from. You're in no position to go throwing orders around. As far as my daughter goes, she is no concern of yours. Mind your business, son."

Casper glanced at a family portrait on the wall opposite the staircase, taken sometime when Shei was approximately in her late teens, and then redirected his attention on Liam again. "I believe her and I have reached a point where she is my business. You see, unlike you, I've established a relationship in what little time I have known her. Therefore, I've got all say in the matter of her well-being. When I inform you that you're not to lay a hand on her, then that's how the cookie crumbles. I'm going to protect her at all costs."

"Your service is no longer requested. You're free to go, Mr. Floyd," Liam snapped angrily.

Casper didn't flinch. "I'm not going anywhere until I know you've backed off."

The defiant remark obviously annoyed Liam because he began marching forward, insinuating that he may be physically prepared to go one on one. "You listen to me and listen now! You are not going to stand here and tell me-"

Casper grabbed the chest area of Liam's button-up

shirt and forcibly jerked him sideways before slamming his back on the wall structuring the staircase. He let go with one hand to reach up and shove his forearm against Liam's throat, crushing his jugular and shutting off the air supply. Since he didn't use his hand to apply pressure, Casper must have been quick minded in decision making because anyone else might not have processed the realization that residual fingerprints were traceable in whatever bruises inflicted.

"You'll not think of hurting her, ever again," Casper grunted.

Liam grabbed his forearm and tried pulling it away but Casper was too stout for him to budge it with both hands.

"Stop this. Get off me," he gasped.

Casper pushed harder. "What kind of scum father dreams of becoming rich by murdering his daughter? Then you turn right around and plot to cut me out of my share. I know you enjoy getting rid of people, but goddamn, did you not think you'd face resistance?"

"All right," Liam said, suffocating. "I'll up your rate. Twenty. Twenty-five. Twenty-five grand."

Casper leaned forward until their faces almost touched. "I think it's a bit late to negotiate. You've got to pay for your lying, greedy ways."

"Thirty thousand," Liam wheezed.

"Fuck!" Casper roared, yanking his arm back from pushing against Liam's throat.

He reached behind Liam and shoved him away from the wall while pulling with the hand still tugging his shirt. Liam stumbled the short distance across the foyer and came to an abrupt stop when striking the side trim of the kitchen doorway. He screeched immediately, and turned toward Casper with one hand covering his nose and mouth.

He staggered backwards slowly into the doorway. "Get out of here. I won't send anyone after you. Just go. You made your point."

Casper faced him. "I don't think I did because you obviously didn't hear me clearly. It's not me that I'm worried about."

"If you're going on about Shei, then you need to get over it. She's had enough garbage in her life that she's got no interest in someone like you. I'll be doing her a favor by giving her nothing more to worry about. As far as my dealings with you go, I'll hand you thirty grand for you to do nothing and walk away. That's it, just walk away," Liam mentioned.

"You don't know when to keep your mouth shut, do you?" Casper inquired, walking slowly toward him. "I don't want as much as a penny from you. There isn't anything you could offer to change my mind. I told her that I was going to protect her and I'm a man of my word. This ends now."

"You've got no idea what you're dealing with, son. I'm capable of bringing charges against you to the extent that I'll put you away for life, and then you'd be in no position to look after anyone. Alfonso would go right along with the plan, so it wouldn't be hard to get you out of the picture. I did it before and I've got no problem doing it again," Liam threatened.

"Alfonso isn't going to do anything if he doesn't have you in his ear," Casper made clear.

"That does it, Mr. Floyd. Walk away before you do something you'll gravely regret," Liam insisted.

Instead of heeding the advice, Casper continued to approach him. "A child and mother's future are at stake here. Not doing something would be my only regret."

Realizing that Casper wasn't withdrawing from coming at him, Liam backtracked into the kitchen. "I don't know what she's told you, but you're out of your damn mind."

"She hasn't told me anything. You've wronged people for too long. Innocent people have had to pay for things they didn't do. Now it's time for someone to put an end to all of this profane injustice," Casper stated, advancing into the doorway.

Trekking farther across the kitchen, Liam unintentionally struck one foot with the other and fell backwards on the floor. Luckily, he landed on his ass and was able to scoot away from Casper persisting to chase.

"Let's not get in over our heads. Everyone is stressed and pissed off. I think it would be good if we calmed down and found another way to handle things," Liam said, trying to persuade him to reconsider his intent.

"I'm calm. If I was pissed, I would have ripped you apart by now," Casper replied.

He looked all around the kitchen. The room housed the basic essentials; oven, microwave, refrigerator, and there were plenty of cabinets and drawers for storing food, dishware, and a variety of cooking supplies. He didn't observe anything that he could actually use to weaponize himself. Really, he didn't need anything. Casper trusted that he could murder him with just his bare hands.

"Don't be irrational. Please, think this through," Liam pleaded.

He dragged himself on the floor until a row of bottom cabinets between the stove and refrigerator stalled his escape, leaving him to terrifyingly witness Casper step closer and closer.

"All right. I'll do what you want. I'll call everything off and forget about it," he said, spewing fright.

Casper smiled sadistically. "Nothing you say makes a difference at this point. I've listened to your lies and played by your rules until I just can't anymore. I'm not the guy you've made me out to be."

"I'll pay you to walk away," Liam uttered.

The primitive mentality to ensure his survival became Casper's driving force. Without taking time to reflect on his thoughts, he raised one foot backwards off the floor and swung his leg forward. Liam howled when the knee plowed straight against his face. Blood gushed out of his nostrils and it didn't take up to a minute for his nose to bruise and begin swelling.

Liam patted under his nose with two fingers and then looked at his blood on them. "You can bet your ass you are going to pay for this. I'll make sure you never see the light of day," he mentioned, trembling all over.

Casper rammed that same knee in his face once more. Liam groaned again. Pulling back, Casper saw that his second effort caused the most severe damage. Liam's nose wasn't only spurting blood but his top and bottom lip was busted as well. The entire lower portion of his face was bloodied, and the violent mess dripped onto his shirt.

Thinking quickly, Casper started opening drawers

above Liam's head. He jerked three of them open before chancing upon various dish rags and towels. Taking one towel from the last drawer before closing all three, he went around their handles with the cloth - hoping it erased fingerprints.

He opened the far left overhead cabinet and found multiple sets of glass dinnerware. "You don't give a man much to choose from," he said indirectly.

Liam was in no shape to speak, of course. He was busy groaning while holding his face.

Casper removed a plate from the cabinet and brought it down fast on the edge of the counter above Liam. Shards of glass dispersed everywhere but the portion he held was largely intact. The long edge away from his hand was jagged. As if knowing what he planned to do already, he set the fractured piece on the counter.

He bent over and grabbed Liam's bloody shirt. Trying to hoist him on his feet was difficult because Liam was uncooperative, and Casper almost lost his grip a few times since the shirt was slick with blood. However, he did manage to bring him off the floor and upright.

"I'm sorry!" Liam wailed painfully.

Casper turned him to face the cabinet and tugged his back against him. Then he reached across the top of Liam's face and used his forearm to pull the back of his head upon his shoulder. Afterwards, he retrieved the broken plate.

Liam gasped.

Then groaned.

Casper's murderous mindset generated him to lift the serrated edge of the glass against Liam's throat.

Suddenly, he sliced flesh with one quick swipe and opened Liam's neck from one side to the other. An incredible amount of blood gushed forth, spraying upon the countertop and sprinkling sections of the wall behind it. Blood continued to pour from the gash, dyeing the majority of his shirt red.

Casper kept a strong grasp of the body, feeling the drainage of life cause Liam to convulse with pain. There wasn't much of anything else he could do, except make gurgling sounds while choking on blood bubbling inside of the gash across his throat.

Casper let go of the broken plate and it went straight to the blood speckled floor, breaking into three parts. He kissed Liam on the side of the face, and smiled.

"You know, I got to thinking about something, and after a while, it started to make a lot of sense. We do what is reasonable and beneficial for our lives, right? So here's what I gathered, and hang on long enough to hear me out. Why would I want to end the life of someone like your daughter - who is naturally drawn to the shady past kind of guy, such as myself? There are just so many opportunities with that one. Love. Equality. Commitment. Sex. Marriage, possibly. But on top of all that, I'm thinking you've got a policy of your own. Probably for the same amount that your wife had insured. Now here's where it gets good. I'm thinking you've got it all willed to your daughter, and that's the perfect catch to me," he explained.

A grisly impression stole his identity. The true nature of his being, which he managed to eclipse for so long, came forward to take pleasure in his carnage.

Finally, Casper Floyd - the monster - was on the

cusp of acquiring all of the wants he ever fantasized.

CHAPTER TWENTY-ONE

"Mommy, I don't like peas," Sierra complained, snarling at her plate of food while sitting alone at the small, round four-person dining table. "They're gross. Girls aren't made to eat them."

"They're good for you, honey," Shei stated, standing with her back to the table and preparing another plate. "The Incredible Hulk loves peas. They make him super strong and green. Don't you want to be like him?"

"No!" Sierra exclaimed quickly. "Peas don't turn him green. People hurt him and he changes. He don't eat anything."

Shit, Shei expressed, working her mouth without producing sound. Then she sighed. "Sounds like you watch TV way too much, little girl."

Sierra giggled, and reached for her glass of sweet tea. "I love TV."

Shei grinned, and turned toward the table with the plate in hand. "I know you do," she said, stepping away from the oven and setting the plate on the left side of the table in front of Sierra. "Sweetheart, I want you to be good for mommy's friend, okay?"

Sierra placed the glass back down on the table after taking a large gulp. "Does he have any powers?"

Shei thought for a moment. She wasn't sure about

how she should answer the question because Sierra was a bit strict when it came to liking people based on their imaginary abilities. "He must have something because he saved mommy from a lot of bad things happening."

"Spiderman shoots stuff. Superman flies. What does your friend do?" Sierra asked.

"Umm- He's nice," Shei answered, and was uncertain if the child was going to buy the response.

"Nice people don't fight," Sierra claimed, sounding disheartened.

"Of course they do," Shei retaliated, turning her back on her daughter and returning to the stovetop to prepare a third plate. "If they weren't nice, then they wouldn't help so many people. Saving people from danger is the nicest thing anyone can do."

"What did I miss?!" Casper asked, emerging inside of the archway between the living room and kitchen. Apparently, he just finished taking a shower since his hair was damp and disheveled. The clothes he put on afterwards could not have been his decision because this wasn't the style he sported over the past several days. This evening he was wearing baggy white shorts that ended below the knees and an NBA jersey representing a team he'd never heard about. Maybe they belonged to Shei's ex-boyfriend who didn't take all of his things after the split.

"My little lady there was asking what superpower you possess," Shei stated, keeping her back toward the room.

"Superpower," he said, slipping into the kitchen and walking to the right side of the table which would be Shei's left if she turned and confronted them. He stepped next to the chair before looking down at Sierra and smiling. "What superpower do you think I have?"

Sierra didn't acknowledge him in any way. She stared at her plate, scrunched her brows, and frowned, as if he was going to have to go through hell in order to be recognized. Obviously, she wasn't the type of kid that openly welcomed someone.

"I told her that you have the ability to be nice," Shei mentioned, while dumping a medium size serving of mashed potatoes on her dish.

"Really?" he asked, pulling his chair out from under the table.

"Yeah, but she said that doesn't count," Shei added.

He sat down and leaned toward Sierra. "What if I told you that I can give you whatever you want?"

She acted a bit reluctant before asking, "Like wishes?"

He nodded. "Kinda. I don't do it all the time. Only for people that are very special."

Sierra shrugged, and rolled her eyes over at him without turning her head. "It's not really a superhero but I don't know anybody else that can do that."

"Want me to prove it to you? Tell me something you want. Anything. I'll make it yours," he encouraged.

She drew her lips together and sideways, taking a moment to think. "I want a Batman cape."

"Hmm," he sounded out, surprised that she wanted something realistically simple. He didn't think this would be difficult to pull off. Maybe Shei had a black bed sheet stashed away that he could cut down to a smaller size and tie two ends together for it to fit over her head. Sierra would never know the difference. She was only seven years old - of course she'd believe him. "A Batman cape it is then. Will take me a little time to get it to you. Maybe tomorrow. I've got to go to a far away world to get it. Plus you aren't allowed to see me work my magic. It wouldn't work if you did."

He seemed to know the words that would perk her interest immediately. Finally, she raised her head and looked over at him directly, grinning sillily with eyes wide open. "Really?! You can do that?!"

He laughed at her voluminous excitement. "Yes, ma'am. I sure can. I'll have it before you can even ask me where it is."

Quickly, she squirmed with incitement. "Mommy! He's getting me a Batman cape!"

Shei giggled quietly. "I heard," she replied cheerily. "See… Didn't I tell you he is magical?"

Sierra looked at him again, and leaned toward him, eager to learn more. "Can you make my peas go away?" she whispered.

He glanced at his plate and saw that he had a decent size serving of everything; mashed potatoes, shredded barbeque roast beef, and the dreaded peas. Then he checked Sierra's plate, noticing that she only had as little as four spoonfuls worth of peas. He didn't really want hers but realized how this might be the most influential way to win her over.

He put his finger over his lips which signaled for her to not say anything, then he lowered it and whispered back, "I can make them disappear but you can't watch me."

Sierra placed one hand against her mouth to keep

from giggling aloud. She was afraid that any sound might draw her mother's attention and cause him to not put his special ability to use. "Cover your eyes," he whispered.

She didn't waste time putting both hands over her eyes. He was surprised that she didn't separate her fingers to sneak a peek at what he was about to do. Evidently she really wanted those peas to go missing.

He reached across and picked up her plate carefully, then pulled back and held it above his own. He was very adamant about not making a sound because the trick was to convince her that he actually could make them vanish. Instead of using silverware to scrape them onto his plate, because that would likely create quite a bit of noise, he laid the side of his hand on the plate and cuffed it around the tiny mound of peas.

He glimpsed at her to make sure she wasn't peeping, and, impressively, she wasn't.

Shei turned just in time to see him sneak the plate back down in front of Sierra. She didn't say anything. Actually, she smiled and pretended she didn't witness the ordeal. The situation was cute to her, and heartwarming in a sense. This was the first positive interaction Sierra ever had with a man since her piece of shit sperm donor never had anything to do with her. Casper's natural ability to get her smiling and chuckling meant a great deal to Shei, and reminded her of the reason she considered taking a chance on him in the first place. His remarkable potential filled her with hope and admiration, which was astounding since she spent many years feeling desolate, emotionally. He no longer needed to prove anything, because she was wholeheartedly convinced that he was a genuinely thoughtful, empathetic man. Exactly the type she didn't perceive to exist.

"Okay. Open your eyes," he whispered down at Sierra.

She uncovered her eyes and stared upon the plate. A half smile pulled across one side of her face as she just sat there in total awe. "How'd you do that?" she asked enthusiastically, while marveling over the small bare spot between the shreds of roast beef and gob of mashed potatoes.

He reached both hands out above the table with his palms turned upward, and shrugged. "I just pointed at them and they disappeared. That's how my magic works."

"But where did they go?" she questioned.

Casper scratched the back of his head. He didn't anticipate an interrogation. "Well- They went to a special place full of things no one wants."

She strained her brows. "No one wanted their cape?"

He laughed. This kid was tough. "No. No. The cape is in another place. A world where all the superheroes live."

Her excitement returned after hearing just the last couple of words. "Wow. Really?"

"Yep," he replied, giving a quick wink.

Shei set her plate on the table and then sat down across from Casper. She looked at him, squinching her eyes to try hiding the glint she knew might be noticeable in them. Positive energies thick with emotion erupted inside of her but didn't give any preliminary warning. She almost declared having a sensational warmth and occasional cold tingles surge throughout her body. Nostalgia. Adoration.

Excitement. Calmness. Satisfaction. All of these emotions, and things unexplained, sent her into an optimistic frenzy. Suddenly, she realized she felt this way - emotionally entwined, butterflies in the stomach, and bodily weightlessness - every time she looked at him.

"Mommy!" Sierra yelled, interfering with her enjoyment of hovering on cloud nine. "Look! I eat my peas. All gone."

She glanced briefly at Sierra's dish. "I see," she commented, seemingly half enthused after having her particularly rare vibe disrupted. "Good job, sweetheart."

She focused on Casper once more, trying to reel in the intensity of emotions she felt just seconds ago, but none affected her the same.

Casper glimpsed at Sierra.

Then he looked at Shei.

Everything about the situation was surreal, and he wanted to visually absorb all details. A week ago he was imagining revenge - taking the diary public and making certain that everyone involved in his misguided prosecution got their day of judgment. Today he delivered a greater form of vengeance - didn't only rid the community of ultimate deception, but shared and continued to exhibit an intimate interest alongside the daughter of that particular villain.

He thought briefly about how screwed up his life was before this moment. Out of all the vile things he did in life, just one memory came forth and played in his mind as he stared across at Shei smiling and flirting with him by way of her eyes.

The hammer clicked when cocked back in position.

The young man on the receiving end of the Glock squirmed uncomfortably on the couch. His tired, apologetic eyes fearfully examined the man standing behind the weapon.

"Dude, I'm telling you the truth. Dad took the book as soon as I told him I wrote everything down. He got pissed, telling me I was fucking stupid because I created evidence. I tried telling him it was therapeutic, that I needed to just let it all out somehow, but he wasn't having it. He told me I better never bring that shit up again," he explained.

"Why the fuck did you tell him? I told you to hide that shit. You knew I was coming for it. I went to jail over your stupid ass. You didn't have the balls to come forward with responsibility. Now I've got the chance to clear my name and you go and fuck it up. You've screwed me over every chance you've had," Casper coldly snapped back at him.

"I'm sorry, bro. None of this should have happened. We shouldn't have gone out that night. Or could have taken a different route. Something, man. I'm having a hard time with this shit. Like, there's days I don't want to be here anymore," Dillon confessed.

"Cut out the pity party," Casper retaliated, before taking a step closer and touching the front of the barrel on Dillon's forehead. "You knew what you were doing. Daddy and his buddies couldn't let the working boy take credit for his actions. Saving your reputation was the reason for everything."

"Bro, I'm sorry. I'm being legit. I never wanted-"

"Stop! You can't say anything that'll change what's

happened." Casper nudged the gun forward which sent Dillon leaning against the backrest, and further thrust the weapon until he laid his head over the top of the couch. "I want to know where the diary is. I'm not here to discuss anything else."

Dillon raised his hands but didn't go anywhere near the gun. "I told you, bro, dad took it," he reaffirmed.

"Then what did he do with it?" Caspser asked.

"I don't know. He probably stashed it away in the lock box. You know that's where he puts everything he doesn't want me getting my hands on," Dillon expressed.

"Lock box. The one behind the French portrait?" Casper inquired, apparently knowledgeable of the safe place Dillon referenced.

"Yeah. I haven't checked but that's got to be where it is. I would take it but my ass would be grass if he looked to see if I touched it. That's a lot different than us getting in there to snatch a little weed," Dillon stated.

"Don't you worry. You're not going to do anything to upset daddy. I'm going to get it myself. Not today, but I'll get it. Right now, I can't go making everything look too obvious," Casper mentioned.

"What do you mean, bro?" Dillon questioned instantly.

Casper pulled the gun from pressing his forehead and pushed it against the soft spot between his chin and throat. "Let's get one thing clear, Dillon. I am not your bro. I may have been years ago but not anymore. That shit was ruined on the day I went to jail. The only thing I see you as being is a lying, two-faced bastard like your father and his asshole prosecutor. You're all pathetic, and you're all going to get what's coming to you."

"Casper, man, wait a minute. I know you're angry but you don't know the full story. I tried talking them into not locking you up. Dude, you've got to believe me," Dillon stressed.

"Oh, Dillon. You didn't try to do anything. You and I both know you changed after starting up your own business, and you weren't going to do anything that tarnished your future. Hell, every time I looked back at you sitting in the front row of the courtroom, you bowed your head in guilt of watching me take the fall for your bullshit," Casper admitted.

"Nah, man. It ain't nothing like that. I've lived with sadness and regret every single-"

A lone, deafening blast ricocheted after Casper pulled the trigger. The force of the bullet penetrating Dillon's neck caused his whole body to jerk while staying seated. Blood poured from the fatal wound, drenching his shirt.

Casper waited a short while for the ringing in his ears to stop. "Hmm. Well, now you don't have to worry about living, period."

He reached his other hand inside the bottom of his shirt before drawing the gun toward him, gripping the barrel with his clothed fingers. Then he slipped his other hand into the bottom of the shirt and used the fabric to wipe the handle and trigger. Trusting that he cleared his prints, Casper grabbed Dillon's right hand and brought it forward. He put the gun in Dillon's hand and situated one of his fingers around the trigger. Afterwards, he reached down slowly and set Dillon's hand between his legs.

He smirked at Shei. "You better be the real deal, because I've gone through nothing but crazy shenanigans to get this far."

She giggled straightaway, and waved her hand over the table at him. "Back it up there, big boy. Actually, it's you who better be legit. I've had nothing but heartache and cannot take it anymore."

He stretched out his leg under the table and tapped her with his foot. Then he grinned, reaching for his glass of water. "Sounds like we've both got some proving to do."

Shei smiled. "Yes, we do."

He neared the glass to his mouth but hesitated. "Speaking of having to prove something… What's the story going to be when everyone starts coming with questions? You know it's just a matter of hours."

"We'll tell them the truth. We went out of town for a couple of nights. A nice little romantic getaway for two. As far as what happened while we were away, must have been some hooligan with a past conviction that had a personal vendetta," she replied.

He chuckled. "Funny. But really, what are we going to say?"

She raised one brow at him. "That is what we're going to say. It isn't like I actually know what happened, so all that I've got to offer is speculation. Plus you did say you know people in high places that are attached to the mess and aren't going to risk outing themselves."

He took a sip of water and returned the glass on the table. "Very true. Sounds like you've really thought this through."

"Oh, I have. I started thinking of an alibi the moment you told me that I was a target," she said.

"Mommy, what's an alibi?" Sierra asked, squirming in her seat. "Is that what you tell me at bedtime?"

"Definitely not, sweetheart. That's a lullaby," Shei answered promptly, giving Casper the split-second playfully panicked expression upon realizing that little ears were picking up on key components within their conversation.

"Then what's alibi?" Sierra inquired.

"You better start eating if you want that cape," Casper intervened.

Sierra turned and stared at him, frowning. Obviously, she wasn't impressed with his response.

"No, Sierra!" Shei scolded her. "Be nice. He is right. If you don't start eating what's on your plate, then I'm not going to let him go anywhere to find you a cape."

Sierra twisted forward, and reached for her fork. "Y'all are mean."

Shei glanced at Casper.

He was looking at her.

She felt that they just shared something incredible. Teamwork. Parental guidance, actually. He got straight to the point with Sierra, however, he was surprisingly polite with his delivery. He just met the child and knew how to deal with her already. This meant a lot to Shei, because she wanted a man in her life that was capable of taking over the responsibilities of being a father for her daughter.

Keeping him in her gaze, Shei scooted her foot across and slid it up slowly between his legs. Her smile broadened. "How about, when all of this blows over, we take a trip? All three of us."

"Like a legit getaway?" he asked.

"Yeah. We could go to the beach. Or rent a cabin in Tennessee. I don't care where we go, honestly. The only thing that matters is that we start making memories with each other," she replied.

Casper sensed he knew where things were going but it didn't phase him that they were headed there quickly. Shei Rivera was too beautiful to pass up - in appearance and personality. She had insecurities regarding men, but, truthfully, that was every woman that wasted her time in failed relationships with men that didn't appreciate and respect them. He believed that her desperation gave him a slight advantage because whatever positive attention she received from a man would be something she clinged onto with hopes that the stars had aligned.

"I like the idea. Let's plan something," he answered.

Warm tingles spilled all over her at once. This was certainly everything she ever wanted. A man who cared, expressed appreciation, and was family oriented. Although they met only a few days ago, Shei had this gut feeling that this was the beginning of something longterm and beneficial.

"I know we crossed paths because of some dire circumstance, but I truly think we were meant to find each other," she stated.

He nodded in agreement. "Yeah. I can see where

that would be the case. I knew there was something special about you the moment I saw you."

Of course he saw something spectacular after she was hauled out of the trunk of the car with a filthy rag tied around her mouth. He recognized options. Fifteen thousand dollars to murder her, or spare her life in exchange for targeting the kingpin while gambling with the notion that two million dollars was at stake. Ultimately, he made the wise decision but could not fill her in on the brutal truth since his situational interest in her saved him from becoming a victim as well. Therefore, he believed it was best to let her stay convinced that she lured him with pure attraction. At the same time, however, she was the most beautiful woman to have ever given him the time of day; so he viewed this as a win from every angle.

Shei sighed lovingly, feeling all of her positive emotions churn and transition into a passion hungering for him. All of her past regrets and negative inflictions melted away.

Casper couldn't lie to himself, he did feel a few fond developments, but it was too soon to put a label on it all. The one thing he did accept was how this was unlike anything he ever experienced.

Continuing to hypnotize each other in a stare - long unflinching - they lost sight of the chaos, violence, deception, unlawful practices that catalyzed this unique partnership.

Quite simply, they were addicted to and immersed in each other's presence.

Regardless of his short term denial.

HER ONLY
FAN
ANDRE SANDERS

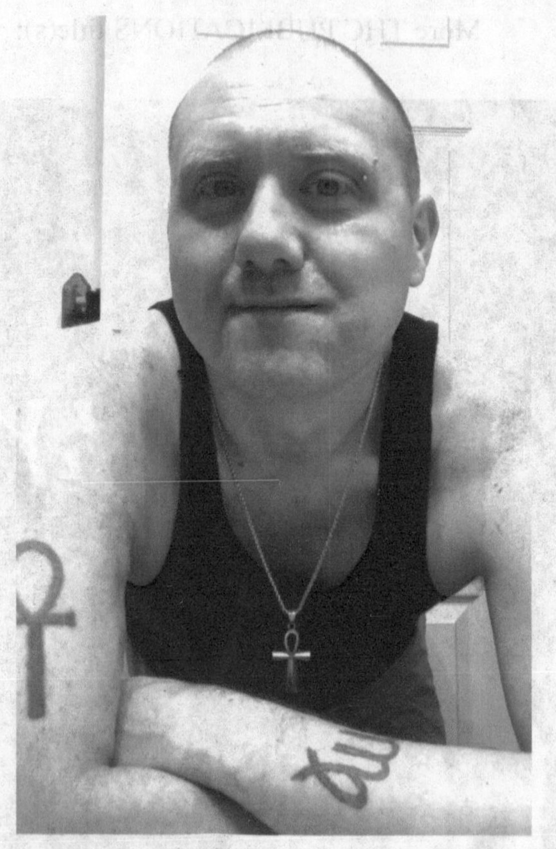

Andre Sanders is an author residing in Christiansburg, VA. Prior to OBJECTION, he published an erotic thriller HER ONLY FAN under the THC Publications imprint. His splatterpunk revenge short story HEN HOUSE became an Amazon bestseller upon release. His second novel TAKER was adapted into a screenplay. All of his titles can be found on Amazon, while HER ONLY FAN is available everywhere books are sold.

Andre is set to begin his next book. Feel free to look him up and follow on Facebook.